"Tell me about Peter," he said

Gavin sat back on the chesterfield, watching her.

"There isn't much to tell," Sophy replied. "Before I came here I was going around with a man called Peter." Quickly she went over the events that had brought her here. "What do you think Peter would think of me now?"

"I think you should forget him." He drew her close, her head against his shoulder. He stroked her hair and her cheek, and his touch on her hair was like sweet fire. He brushed the nape of her neck with his lips, and she felt the impact pierce her whole body.

"I could make you forget him." Gavin's voice was husky. And if his mouth closed on hers, Sophy knew, nothing could reach her. He would make her forget her own name. . . .

JANE DONNELLY
is also the author of these
Harlequin Romances

These books may be available at your local bookseller.

For a free catalog listing all titles currently available,
send your name and address to:

HARLEQUIN READER SERVICE
1440 South Priest Drive, Tempe, AZ 85281
Canadian address: Stratford, Ontario N5A 6W2

Face the Tiger

Jane Donnelly

Harlequin Books

TORONTO • NEW YORK • LONDON
AMSTERDAM • PARIS • SYDNEY • HAMBURG
STOCKHOLM • ATHENS • TOKYO • MILAN

Original hardcover edition published in 1983
by Mills & Boon Limited

ISBN 0-373-02576-9

Harlequin Romance first edition October 1983

Printed in U.S.A.

CHAPTER ONE

THERE had never been a time when Sophy Wade had not been in love with Peter Fisher. Right back in her earliest memories he had been her hero, her dream. She had always done a lot of dreaming, it was the thing she was best at. It irritated her family. 'For God's sake stop mooning around,' her mother would say when Sophy curled up in a window seat, a book on her knee and her wide green-grey eyes fixed on some inner world, and Sophy would jump guiltily and look around for something to do more in keeping with the kind of younger daughter her parents had wanted and expected.

Although she suspected they hadn't expected her at all. With Nicholas and Cressida their family had been complete. Sophy was surely an accident and she had gone on being an embarrassment—the odd one out from the start.

Her mother was still saying, smiling, every time she had to introduce Sophy to anyone, 'How her father and I came to produce this one we'll never know!' Her mother was beautiful, slim and graceful as a ballet dancer, with hardly a line on her face. Sophy was a tall girl with a round face and fine fair hair that resisted attempts to style it. At the hairdressers they compared her hair with her mother's sleek dark tresses and sister Cressida's rich chestnut mane, so that usually Sophy did her own shampooing and only went near the professionals when she was in desperate need of a haircut. She had only tried doing that for herself once, when she had made such a mess of it that Jenny—of

5

Jennifer and Jeremy, *the* hairdressing salon in this Northern town—nearly had hysterics.

Sophy's hair needed cutting now. Her fringe was falling in her eyes as she stood in the office at the back of the antique shop, peering through the glass panels at Sara Wade selling a Victorian doll to a woman who might be going to take it home and cherish it, or could just as easily be another dealer. The customer was upending the doll, looking for signs that this was a genuine Jumeau, and because it was, Sophy's mother would stick to the very high price asked and possibly get it.

This doll was one of Sophy's favourites. There was a cabinet of them and because they were rare the cabinet was never full, and few dolls stayed for long. Sara Wade had a name for dolls, although she was an expert in china too, and sharply knowledgeable about most antiques, from jewellery to furniture.

Sophy knew beauty when she saw it, some of the things in here left her quite breathless with wonder, but there was really no place among valuable antiques—and certainly not in her mother's shop—for a girl who had sent an early Wedgwood vase spinning when she was fourteen and would never be allowed to forget it.

Sometimes Sophy did some of the business typing, but only when Cressida was too busy. Cressida was a fast and accurate typist, and she worked here. She was here now, wearing a tan silk shirt and matching skirt that brought out the red glints in her hair. Her hair was long, just over her shoulders, and it waved beautifully back, making her look like a girl from one of those T.V. sagas about the very rich.

Sophy's hair never fell that way. Sophy could never have reached into the cabinet and brought out another doll, and handled it so confidently and discussed the finer points with her mother and the woman who had to be a dealer, like Cress was doing now. Sophy had always envied Cressida. She had loved her because Cress was a super sister, just as Nick was a marvellous brother, and Sara and Gilbert Wade were almost ideal parents.

It was the fault of none of them that they were all so talented and so good-looking, when Sophy was neither. Until recently what-are-we-going-to-do-with-Sophy had been a problem. She had left school with three average O-levels and gone to the local Polytechnic for a secretarial course. After that she could at least type her father's books. Then she had taken cooking, and she wasn't bad at that, but her mother was better.

When Sophy was asked what she did she said, 'I fetch and carry.' There weren't many jobs around now unless you were qualified or exceptional, but Sophy kept busy. She did the garden, she helped in the house. She baby-sat for friends, and did anything her family asked her to do, and basked in the glow of their love; and took it for granted that occasionally they would look at her with exasperation because they *were* superior. Any fool could see that.

Sophy's future would have been secure. The family was prosperous, both parents successful, Nick with a good second class law degree, getting established as a solicitor, and Cress married last year to the son of the owner of a large store in the middle of town. And they all loved Sophy and would have looked after her if the need had arisen, but they were delighted and relieved when Peter Fisher started dating her.

She had had other boys calling round and phoning up, but Sophy was a one-man girl, even before that man realised she was no longer wearing braces on her teeth. Nicholas and Peter were the same age, twenty-five. They had been friends, through school and college, Peter had been coming to the house for years, and Sophy had always adored him.

It was a family joke. A lot of things about Sophy were a family joke. Until she was about ten she had reacted like an affectionate puppy when Peter was around, and because Nick Wade was his best friend and he had no brothers and sisters of his own. Peter had been quite flattered by the devotion of Nick's kid sister.

He was her dream hero then, slaying monsters and riding between the stars with her, but as she grew into her teens the pictures changed. She tried to hide her feelings. she no longer ran to him, although they all knew she still had a crush because she blushed if he looked straight at her. She denied it, and dreamed of his lovemaking, tender and sweet, and none of the other boys she met ever stood a chance.

Peter was doing well in the local branch of an engineering company, a member of the same country club as the Wades. He and Nick played squash together there, and Cress and her husband Rob often joined them. They all seemed to Sophy to be demon players, leaping around the court, eyes and wrists co-ordinating. She was shortsighted as well as having— according to her family—two left feet. She couldn't follow the flight of the ball half the time, much less hit it; and it was the same with tennis. But she could swim.

In the water she became as graceful as Cress, and swifter and stronger, and it was in the pool that Peter blinked the water out of his eyes and took his first real hard look at her. Sophy usually came here mornings when there were few swimmers. In the twelve months the club had been open this was the first time they had met in the pool, or he had seen her in a swimsuit.

She always wore loose-fitting clothes because she

was convinced that her body was top-heavy. Cress and Sara were small-breasted, and wore wide belts accentuating their tiny waists, but in the winter Sophy went around in sloppy sweaters pulled down over her jeaned hips and in the summer it was caftans in various materials and colours.

But in the pool that day there was no real concealment, in a skimpy black bikini, and Peter, swimming in the deep end, saw her emerge from the sauna and walk towards the showers, as though he was seeing her for the first time. Her legs were long and slim, stomach flat and her breasts absolutely right for her height. He was impressed. She hadn't noticed him and when she came back he hauled himself out and went to meet her, and was amused and pleased to see the colour rise in her cheeks. With her wet skin glowing she looked almost pretty, and she always had had a beautiful complexion.

They had a snack together afterwards, in the bar by the pool, and when Nick turned up later he was surprised to find them cosily seated side by side sipping iced lager and finishing off two plates of lasagne.

Sophy couldn't believe her luck. She had never had Peter to herself before. Except in dreams, of course. She sat and listened, drinking in his words, her eyes lingering on his face as though he was the Mona Lisa. She had never dared stare before, or sit as close as this and look just at him, but she could this afternoon, although when Nick appeared she sat back and said, 'I ought to be off, I only meant to stay about half an hour.'

Nick had a flat at home. The attics had been converted for him when he came down from university, and when he came back that night he looked into the drawing room where Sophy was sitting alone, listening to a cassette of Barbra Streisand, and said 'I've got something to tell you.'

'Tell me?' Please let it be about Peter, and please let it be nice.

'Peter says you're a fantastic listener.'

Peter had talked about his job. He was ambitious, and Sophy thought that was wonderful and she could have listened to him for ever. 'I'll take you along to the club with me,' Nick said kindly, 'when old Pete's there.'

'I couldn't do that.'

'Of course you could. You've always fancied him, haven't you?' He seated himself, a charming elegant young man, with the assurance of one whose moments of self-doubt were few and far between. 'Well, if I'm any judge he's beginning to fancy you.'

'I don't believe you.'

'And Pete Fisher,' Nick went on judicially, 'wouldn't be a bad catch at all.'

Sophy had never expected to 'catch' Peter. She wouldn't have known how to start. She lacked Cressida's gay wiles that enchanted every man within her orbit, but Nick helped, watching benevolently when Sophy sat worshipping at Peter's feet. Cress and Robin approved too. Everyone thought it was lovely that Peter was taking Sophy around and Sophy's dreams began to spill into real life.

She still lacked confidence in almost every way, but if Peter liked her enough to date her she had to be doing something right, although she couldn't for the life of her think what it was.

She had walked into the shop this morning to see if her mother, or Cress, wanted any shopping done. She had to collect a suit from the cleaners for Nick, and a ream of typing paper for her father, and Sara Wade had made several additions to the list before leaving Sophy with a cup of instant coffee in the office.

The coffee was drunk now, and as soon as the customer left with a doll, prettily boxed in a cradle of tissue paper, Sophy emerged. Maybe she imagined that her mother and sister always frowned slightly while she threaded her way between the treasures, and always let out little sighs of relief when she reached the door without elbowing anything off its stand. If they did she couldn't blame them. She knew she was accident-prone around anything fragile.

'See you later, dear'; said her mother.

'You are getting your hair done, aren't you?' said Cress. 'You do want Peter to be proud of you.'

'Oh *yes*!' said Sophy fervently. She desperately wanted Peter to be proud of her, and she had an appointment at the hairdressers in half an hour. Tonight was an occasion, a gala charity dinner-dance, and she had a new dress too, and ever since Peter had told her he'd bought her her ticket she had been walking on air.

Cressida and Nicholas had always had a very full social life. Cressida was twenty-three now, to Sophy's nineteen, and since she married Robin she had lived in a mock-Georgian mews; but when she did live at home it seemed to Sophy that she never spent an evening in. The same with Nick. They had tried sometimes in the last two years to take Sophy along with them, to parties, to group outings, but shyness made her awkward company. She knew she was a drag, and when she made excuses they never pressed her. So Sophy didn't get out much. She had friends of her own that she had made at school and Poly, but on the whole they were not exciting folk.

Peter was exciting. He made her heart race every time he smiled at her, and he was almost as handsome as Nick, with regular features and a ready smile. Going to the charity dinner-dance as Peter's partner tonight was just about the most exciting thing that had ever happened to Sophy, because tonight she would be on show as his girl. They had been around together now for two months and three days—the date he first asked her to have dinner with him would be engraved on her heart for ever; and tonight was terribly important, because she would be meeting not only people she already knew but business colleagues of Peter's.

Peter had talked to her about them. He was a go-getter who intended making his way to the top. The man who was guest speaker tonight was the kind of man that Peter aimed to be, and Peter was so clever that Sophy had no doubt at all he would finish on the board of directors. She admitted several times that she lacked his brains and then he would tell her that it didn't matter and she would melt with longing, wanting him to make love to her.

He hadn't, yet. He had kissed her and said she was so sweet, and she went limp with delight under the pressure of his lips and hands, but a little scared at what must happen next, quite soon. She wouldn't have resisted, she *loved* him, but so far it had ended with the kiss and the touch.

She had bought a new dress for tonight, extravagantly romantic in white, with frills and ruffles, and she was now on her way to have her hair styled to match, for tonight was a kind of test, more important than any other exam she had ever taken.

She didn't expect to shine. Cressida and Robin were going to the dance too and Sophy knew that Cress would outshine her, because she always did without even trying. But Sophy would look as beautiful as possible so that Peter wasn't ashamed of her, and she was a good listener and not a bad dancer. Today some of the euphoria had started ebbing away, and unless she kept a close guard on herself, apprehension might be creeping in.

She wasn't good at first impressions, and tonight there would be lots of introductions, when the élite of the local business world gathered under the glittering chandeliers of the town hall's banqueting room. Cress and Rob would know most of them, but Sophy didn't, and although she should get through dinner easily enough she dreaded afterwards, when people were going to say, 'Cressida's *sister*?' or, 'Of course I've met your family,' and through her mind would run idiot retorts like, 'I'm the one they keep in the secret room in the west wing.' 'I'm the ugly duckling', was the simple truth. 'The brains and the beauty got used up for Nick and Cress.' But all she would do was smile and feel her face stiffen.

They greeted her affably at the hairdressers. Cressida was one of their best customers, in twice a week at least and always getting star treatment. Sophy Wade was a nice girl, but she had no glamour, and she rarely got Jennifer or Jeremy. Any assistant who was free took Sophy, and today it was Annie who was still waiting to hear if she had passed her City and Guilds and who said severely, 'My goodness, you need a conditioner!'

'You make me feel like a very old dog,' said Sophy, peering through her fringe, and Annie giggled. 'What I want,' said Sophy, 'is something that will go with a long white broderie anglaise skirt with a peplum jacket.' Her hands fluttered, describing it, and Annie brightened.

'Going somewhere special?'

'To a special dance with a special man,' said Sophy, who had never come in here before asking for anything more than a general tidy-up.

It was the first visit to the hairdressers she had ever

enjoyed. The discussion became animated. Annie brought out trade magazines and they hunted for styles, although Sophy's hair wasn't going to hold anything elaborate. 'You want a light perm,' Annie decided. 'I could do you that if you liked. It would give it some body with plenty of conditioner.'

'You're on,' said Sophy.

When she saw herself in the mirror she was delighted. She couldn't think why she hadn't had something done with her hair before. Cress had asked her from time to time, 'Why don't you try to do something with your hair, Sophy?' So had her mother, sighing, 'Do put your hair back, dear, it can't be good for your eyes.'

But Sophy's reflection now showed a girl with a very pretty hairstyle, softly waved and flipped up at the ends. She *had* to look pretty tonight, and she was beginning to believe that she could, but she knew that she needed all the help she could get.

She was ready and waiting ages before Peter was due to arrive. He was picking up Cress and Robin on the way and they were all four going on together, and Sophy had started preparing as soon as she'd washed up from her father's tea.

The dress had cost a lot of money, but her father had written out the cheque, and when she went downstairs he was the first to see her. She was not his favourite daughter, but he wanted the best for her, and when Sara told him that young Fisher was showing an interest Gilbert Wade was prepared to do his bit to encourage it.

Tonight she looked quite presentable, really quite attractive, and she was a good child. Gilbert Wade taught economics and wrote textbooks and considered that Sophy was a fool, but he believed he loved her. 'You look beautiful,' he told her now. 'Absolutely charming!'

Her mother came into the drawing room and said the same, and after that there was nothing for Sophy to do but sit down, with her skirts spread wide, waiting to be collected, while her parents turned back to their respective interests—he with a book, she with a glossy magazine. The clock ticked the minutes by and Sophy thought it would have been nice to talk, but Nick was out and her mother and father had never really had much to say to her. They brightened up when Cress and Rob and Peter walked in. Gilbert began to pour out sherry, and said, 'Now that really is a cracker of a dress!' to Cress, who laughed and did a twirl-around for them. It was simply but superbly cut, sleeveless and deep-V neck, black silk with glorious clashing colours of gold, peacock blue, purple, scarlet, tangerine, as though someone had splashed them on. It was probably a model. It was very unlikely there would be another like it there tonight, although any number of girls could be in white broderie anglaise dresses.

'And don't *you* look lovely?' said Cressida, as Sophy stood up, 'Hey, look at my little sister!' That was another family joke, because Sophy was a good five inches taller than Cressida. Sophy's eyes were on Peter, his was the reaction that mattered. Her reflection in the bedroom mirror had almost reassured her that she was going to pass tonight's test, but when Peter looked surprised and pleased her heart slipped a beat with joy.

He and Rob were both very distinguished in evening dress, and Sophy said, 'You look just——' floundering for words, making them laugh at her because it was such an endearing giveaway the way she stood there blushing.

Peter smiled at her fondly and said, 'So do you, absolutely just——' and gave her a quick hug and she knew that it could be tonight that he would tell her he loved her. There were stars in her eyes when she went outside with the three of them to get into his car, but there were no stars in the sky. It had been a drab grey day in early spring, although Sophy had been too preoccupied to notice. But now it began to rain, and they hurried down the short drive to the car parked in the roadway. 'I should get in the back with that skirt,' said Cress, diving first into the back seat herself, and Sophy gathered up her skirts and found herself bundled beside Cress, praying that her white hemline was not mud-spattered.

The town hall car park was filling rapidly and Peter had to manoeuvre to find a place as near as possible to the entrance. Even then there seemed quite a way to go, and they ran, arriving in the entrance hall laughing and shaking the rain from their hair. Well, Cress and Rob and Peter laughed and shook off the rain, but Sophy seemed to be wetter than they were. Even with Peter holding her arm her skirts had encumbered her, and she was sure her hair was going to fall out of its style unless she kept her head still.

She wished now she had chosen a less fussy outfit. Cress looked so slim and vital, skin and hair shining from the mist of rain, while Sophy simply felt damp. Rob's parents, Mr and Mrs Turnbull, were there. Cress's mother-in-law greeted Sophy with a kiss, she always felt sorry for Sophy, and father-in-law said in a booming voice, 'Hello, young Sophy, when are you going to stop growing?'

Sophy had been the tallest bridesmaid at Cress's wedding, and Mr Turnbull was a short man who usually asked her this question. He didn't meet her often, but each time he trotted out his stupid joke she resisted the temptation to snap, 'I stopped four years ago, what do you think I am, a freak?'

She smiled now. She was smiling all the time, being introduced to strangers and asking them how they did and then finding it hard to think of anything else to say: being greeted by familiar faces. She was glad when they went in to dinner, because you didn't have to talk while you were eating.

The menu was very good and the wine was pleasant. After a couple of glasses Sophy began to relax, and smiled at the jokes and listened to the chatter of her companions. Peter was pleased with her. He kept her glass filled and his eyes were kind, and he touched her hand and squeezed her arm a couple of times, laying little claims to her that she loved.

She didn't have Cress's looks nor Cress's brains, but she knew that she had a lot to give in devotion and caring. She *could* help Peter. She could make his home so comfortable. At present he lived in a big old furnished flat that he shared with a couple of young men. If he married Sophy she could cook for him and care for him, and perhaps there would be children.

Sophy got on well with children; and with animals, and with old people. Cress was in no hurry to start a family, and her mother said she was wise there because even the best of children were a tie. Cress was young and Robin said he didn't see himself as a father just yet, but Sophy who had said nothing—nobody was asking her opinion anyway—had thought wistfully that she would like nieces and nephews who might be her only chance of children around the house.

But now there was another chance, and while a man at the top table was thanking them for coming on behalf of the charity that would benefit this year, Sophy started dreaming about a house that she was sharing with Peter, the laughter of shadowy children, sunshine streaming in through the windows.

The noise of applause disturbed her dream. Several

speakers had stood up for a few minutes and then sat down to applause, but this clapping was clamorous, before this man had even said a word. He was the guest speaker, his name had been on the tickets: Gavin Tighe.

Peter had talked about him with envious admiration, so Sophy knew that he was head of a one-time small and struggling firm that in spite of the recession had grown into a highly successful enterprise during the last ten years.

Peter had never met Gavin Tighe, but this speech was the high spot of the evening for him, and because of that Sophy had meant to listen intently herself, and the first sight of the man shook her wide awake.

He was well over six foot tall, slim and muscular, with dark hair and dark brows, and in the few moments he stood there, before he began to speak, the power of his personality came over so that there was complete silence, as though everyone in the room held their breath. He could keep them like this, thought Sophy, he could hypnotise them. He looks hard as nails, ruthless as a pirate, that must be how he got where he is, and I hope with all my heart that Peter doesn't turn out like him.

There wasn't all that much difference in age, she had expected Gavin Tighe to be older. And she supposed he was quite handsome, if you liked the dark Satanic type. Cress's lips curved, her tongue ran slowly between them, and Sophy felt a sickness in the pit of her stomach. She could guess what most of the women here tonight were thinking, but he made her so uneasy that she shrank back in her chair, as though those piercing eyes were seeking for her.

Sophy rarely took instant dislikes, and it must have been because Peter had talked about this man as though he was a model of the born survivor. Which he obviously was, and there was nothing wrong with that so long as you hurt nobody. But Gavin Tighe wouldn't let anyone stand in his way. Sophy could imagine him cutting down any poor soul who tried, with savage impatience and without wasting a word. He was the last kind of model she wanted Peter to take.

There was no sign of savagery in him tonight. He had a deep carrying voice and he had his audience in convulsions of laughter. It was a superb after-dinner speech, they were loving it. In his career in industry he had met the kind of difficulties they all understood, but he made them sound hilarious. He told anecdotes about men who were household names, politicians mainly, that were just short of libellous and without exception very funny.

Sophy smiled, of course, but she couldn't peal with helpless laughter like the rest of them because she kept seeing this man wearing another face—the dark brows in the straight line, the mouth grim and set. He would be terrifying if he was angry, she was convinced of it. Heaven help the man, or the woman, he turned on then.

He couldn't even see her. She was at the end of a table a fair way from the top table, and she was sitting back, entirely blocked out by Peter, who had all his attention on the speaker. But she still felt personally threatened. As though—— She gulped more wine because her mouth was dry, and thought, as though I was in a room with a tiger. There's a smile on the face of the tiger, but all I can see are the tiger's teeth.

Her hand might have been shaking. She wasn't used to sherry followed by three glasses of wine, and she was born clumsy and not looking what she was doing. But when she put down her glass she managed to tip it, so that a little spilled on the tablecloth and the rest went on to her lap. In the laughter it went almost unnoticed. Cress rolled her eyes and leaned across and dabbed the spot on the tablecloth with a napkin, while Sophy tried to mop her skirt. Peter turned, and she managed a smile with a little shrug and he grinned back, then went on listening to the speech.

Good job it's white wine, thought Sophy. Good job cotton washes. But it was going to spoil the rest of the evening, because she couldn't get out on the dance floor with a sopping skirt. Cress wouldn't have cared. Cress would have sworn when it happened, but it wouldn't have bothered her. But of course Cress wouldn't have knocked a glass over, and she wouldn't have been dressed in broderie anglaise, like one of the Victorian dolls in the cabinet.

I am a drip, thought Sophy, a soaking wet drip; and she felt more like bursting into tears than laughing.

During the applause at the end of the speech she said to Peter, 'That's the man you want to be like?'

'Who wouldn't?' said Peter. 'And I'll tell you something else, I wouldn't mind working for him.' He said this behind a hand in case any of his colleagues overheard because Tighe Industries was a bigger and rival concern.

'You think he'd make a nice boss?' She could think of nothing worse than to be accountable to that man, and Peter smiled at her as though these were things she couldn't understand.

'He's a winner. You never hear of redundancies in his factories.'

'He probably shackles them to the machines,' she muttered, and Peter's eyebrows rose. He did not associate tartness with Sophy.

'We'll be meeting him afterwards,' he said, and Sophy was almost glad she had spilled the wine because it gave her an excuse to keep in the background, even though it meant not being close to Peter all the time. She would have hated to be ushered forward to shake hands with Gavin Tighe.

This was not turning into the evening she had hoped for, although she couldn't have said she was having a rotten time. She stayed put, at the little table round the edge of the dance-floor that had been allotted to the Turnbulls' party, and her seat was behind a large floral display so that she had to peer through the fronds to get a clear view of the dancers. But a lot of the time Peter sat with her, and on and off so did Cress and Rob, and friends came over to chat. Girl friends mostly, some of whom Sophy baby-sat for, and then the talk was usually about their children.

Peter was star-struck with Gavin Tighe. It was the only word Sophy could find for all this admiration, and she supposed there were some small surface similarities. Peter had dark hair and broad shoulders, but Gavin Tighe was a giant of a man. At least it seemed that way. You could see him over the heads of the rest all the time, without any trouble at all. He didn't seem to do any dancing, but he was always at the centre of the crowd, and Peter came back to the table after talking to him and announced, 'He's the man of the future, you know.'

'I didn't know,' said Sophy, 'but I'll bet he's a man with a past.' She didn't mean that as a compliment and it came out sounding waspish. The wine was loosening her tongue and she was talking rubbish, because she didn't really know the first thing about him, except that Peter would have liked to be in his shoes and she was not the kind of girl a man like that would look at twice.

If Peter did see himself as another Gavin Tighe there would be no place in his life for Sophy, no dream house and dream children, and she sat back behind the floral arrangement of artificial flowers and sipped another glass of wine.

Peter tried to get her to dance and so did Rob, but apart from her skirt still being limp and damp she wasn't too sure by now that she would be steady on her feet, so she said she always trod on her partner's toes when she danced, and they laughed and let her stay. Cress, getting her alone, gave her a few words of sisterly advice. 'Are you enjoying yourself?'

'Of course I am.'

'Why are you hiding in the corner here? Why don't you come out and dance? That's what you ought to be doing.'

'My skirt's wet,' said Sophy, 'and I think I've drunk too much wine.'

'I give up!' sighed Cressida. 'Anyhow, so long as you're happy.'

I am happy, Sophy told herself, and after Gavin Tighe left she began to enjoy the evening more. She asked Peter, 'Shall you be seeing him again?' and Peter looked puzzled.

'I don't suppose so—why?'

'I wondered if he might be offering you a job.'

'Good lord, no!' And the emphasis wasn't because someone else might overhear, that was the truth, there had obviously been no question of that, but it had been worrying Sophy. She had had visions of Peter moving away and coming back in a year of two, ruthless and successful and out of reach. She was really quite happy for the rest of the evening, and altogether the charity dance was a great success.

She sat with Cress in the back of the car again going home, and it would have been lovely if Peter had dropped Cress and Rob off first and then taken Sophy home. He might have come in for a last cup of coffee, and she had hoped he would tell her that he had enjoyed the evening so much more because she was with him. That was when she had hoped he would take her in his arms, and really kiss her, and say that because it was so good when they were together he wanted her with him all the time.

Marriage was what she craved, but if Peter had said, 'I love you, come and live with me,' she would have braved her parents' disapproval, because she wanted Peter more than a gold band on her finger. But it was very late, and her heart sank when she realised they were taking the route that brought them to her house first.

Cressida was saying that one of the women had told her there was an article about Gavin Tighe in a magazine this week. 'I'm getting that tomorrow,' she said, teasing Rob. 'If I went in for pin-ups I'd stick him on the wall. Or the ceiling, over the bed.'

'Not over my bed,' said Rob, and Sophy thought, what an awful thought, and said, 'She doesn't mean it.'

'Don't you be so sure!' Cress gurgled. 'Anyhow, I shall get the magazine and I'll bring it round for you. You're a single girl, you stick his picture on your ceiling.'

I'd rather have a springing tiger above me, thought Sophy, and bit her lip because that was exactly the impression she got from Gavin Tighe.

At breakfast her mother wanted to hear all about the dance and Sophy gave them a potted version. She didn't mention the guest speaker, but almost everyone else who had been there, and that the main course had been duckling à l'orange. Her father was behind his newspaper, but she talked to him too, and told them it had been a lovely evening. And it had. She was seeing Peter tonight. When he had left her on her front doorstep last night he'd kissed her and said, 'I'll call round for you about eight o'clock, we might have a Chinese meal.'

That would get her through the day. She did the family wash and managed to get most of the wine stain out of her skirt. She should of course have gone to the cloakroom as soon as it happened and washed it out, the mark had set by now and was proving troublesome around the edges. When Cress looked in, on her way home from the shop, Sophy was sitting at the kitchen table searching for help in an old book of household hints.

Cress put the magazine on the table and asked, 'Are you sure you've never met him before?'

'What are you talking about?' Sophy kept a fingertip on Stain Removal in the index, although when Cress went on, 'Gavin Tighe,' her finger slipped.

'Read this,' Cress tapped the magazine, 'and tell me who you think he's talking about.'

Not about Sophy, of course, and Cress knew that, she was joking. 'Must fly,' she said. 'I only dropped in to give you this. Everything all right?'

Cress wouldn't have been interested in a stain on a skirt, she was moving off as she spoke. 'It was a good night last night, wasn't it?' she said.

'Wasn't it?' Sophy echoed after her, and as the front door closed she opened the magazine.

You could have stuck the photograph up on the wall, Sophy thought sourly; it was big enough, a whole magazine page. Half a dozen men had been interviewed for this article, but the rest had quite small photographs in comparison. Gavin Tighe had been given star billing. The subject was men who were succeeding in spite of modern-day odds, the 'secrets' of their success, with bits of advice and warning for the rest of us.

It was a women's magazine and brightly and lightly written, and they were all asked what part women had played in their struggle for fame and fortune. The three who were married were fulsome about how their wives had supported them, although Sophy recalled that last week the split-up of one of these marriages had been reported. But of course magazine articles were always printed months ahead. She was reading the others first. She wasn't particularly interested in them, but she didn't want to read about Gavin Tighe. The way Cress had grinned there was going to be something upsetting in that piece, because although Cress was kind she didn't know half the time when she was hurting Sophy's feelings. If you were the family clown you were expected to take a joke against yourself even if you didn't think it was funny.

He had a house in Witherstone, a Yorkshire village about twenty miles away from the Lancashire town where Sophy lived, The Old Mill House, where he had entertained the interviewer in a study with panelled walls overlooking lawns and a rushing stream with a little bridge. They had drunk champagne and he had told her that he attributed most of his success to luck.

'Liar,' thought Sophy. Sitting there, knocking back champagne, pretending it's all been a doddle. If I'd been asking the questions I'd have said, 'Come off it! You sound like one of those actresses of fifty who look thirty and say "The only beauty treatment I use is pure soap and water." What kind of fools do you think the public are?'

She looked at his photograph and imagined herself saying just that. This man seemed to bring out a suppressed and surprising aggression in her.

She read on, and this had to be where Cress had said he could have been thinking of Sophy, where he said that the idea of there always being a woman behind a successful man was rubbish. Often as not the woman behind the man was holding him back. Had he a special type of woman in mind that would-be top achievers should avoid? he was asked. And yes, he most certainly had, and he went on to describe her.

He had seen any number of promising men fall for a nest-builder, who clipped his wings and kept him from realising a fraction of his potential. The quiet clinging woman could be a killer of ambition and achievement. Girls who listened and said nothing usually had nothing to say, and the charming dimwit of nineteen would be an insufferable bore at twenty-nine.

He made marriage sound a trap. No, he said, he did not believe in love. He believed in lust, which maintained the excitement of sexual surprise; and if he needed cosseting and care a stay at a health farm. His advice to an ambitious young man was work like hell and steer clear of the love of a good woman.

The reporter seemed to think he was talking tongue-in-cheek, but Sophy did not. She bet he meant every word of it, even if the champagne glasses were clinking while he was holding forth. She noticed he had no word for the ambitious young woman, chauvinistic oaf.

And this was how Cress saw Sophy—a dimwit, a quiet drain on a man because all she had to offer was love; and Sophy supposed Cress could be right. She had never had a high opinion of herself, but Peter had told her he didn't mind her not being as brainy as the rest of the family, and she was acting like an idiot now sitting here shrivelling inside because a man who didn't know she was alive had talked a lot of drivel.

She shut the magazine, dropped it in the kitchen wastebin and let the lid bang down. Then she took it out again, because Cress would very likely want it back and if Sophy said she had thrown it away that would be admitting how much it had goaded her. Of course it hadn't. It had probably been printed just to get readers writing in. She wondered if Peter had read it and until seven o'clock she had meant to take the magazine along on their date this evening. She could show it to him over the meal and he would laugh at it.

But before eight o'clock she had changed her mind. She didn't want to go over it again, she really would rather forget it, and she left it in a drawer in her bedroom. If Peter asked if she'd seen it she would admit she had, but she wasn't bringing up Gavin Tighe's name. He could have spoiled her appetite, and the Green Lantern was one of her favourite restrauants.

She had been here with Peter several times, sitting under the red paper lanterns painted with green dragons, sharing dishes galore, and sipping tiny cups of sake. But tonight something had taken the bounce out of Peter, and in answer to her concerned query, 'Is anything the matter, you look tired?' he admitted,

'I guess I am, it's been a tough day.'

'I'm sorry. We shouldn't have come out. We could have stayed home. I'd have cooked us something.'

'This is hardly a riot of excitement, is it?' he said wryly, and the restaurant was fairly empty for a Saturday night, but the food was good and the service came with smiling faces, and Sophy thought she was enjoying herself.

By the time the coffee was served Peter was looking almost haggard, and she said, 'Maybe you should have an early night. You do feel all right, don't you, you're not sickening for anything?' She put a hand on his forehead. It felt clammy rather than fevered, no temperature at any rate, and he frowned under her light touch, and said,

'There's nothing wrong with me, I'm just tired, but perhaps we ought to call it a day.'

She was in her own bed at half past ten and she didn't sleep very well. She didn't know why, but she woke several times and had difficulty in getting back to sleep. Once the bedclothes were tossed off and she lay on the edge of the bed with her feet on the floor, and she almost panicked recalling her sleepwalking which at one time had been a very real problem.

She hadn't done that for years, she had outgrown the habit long ago, but a faint chilling memory lingered for a moment after she opened her eyes, like fog on a lonely moor, and she sat up and shook herself before lying down to sleep again.

On Sunday morning the household rarely stirred before the Sunday papers fell on the doormat, which was around half past nine. But Sophy, waking at her usual time of eight o'clock, felt a need to be active, and came downstairs and started preparing a picnic. It was going to be a beautiful spring day and she would phone Peter and suggest they go to the Lakes, or anywhere he liked. He had said, 'See you tomorrow,' when he'd left her, without making any firm arrangements, and they would probably have ended at the Country Club with Nick, and possibly with Cress and Rob, and lunched there. But a picnic for two would be nice and she was sure she could get Peter to agree with her.

She raided the fridge and packed a carrier bag, and then wandered out into the garden where the sun was rising in a hazy blue sky and there was a marvellous freshness about everything as though this really was the first morning and she was listening to the first bird. The daffodils were out and the lawn looked like green velvet. Sophy loved her garden; she spent a lot of time out here. Walking the lawn barefoot, when the dew was on it, was the nearest thing to the delight of squelching the sand of a wet beach through your toes as a child.

She kicked off her slippers now and walked down as far as the hazelnut tree with the hole at the top of the trunk where the squirrel lived. If you sat under this tree quietly for a long time the squirrel would sometimes come out, and in the winter she had seen him stealing titbits from the bird table.

Nick's kitchen door was ajar, up there under the eaves, a dark opening like the squirrel's home; and if she climbed the outside iron steps she could cadge a cup of coffee, because the first thing Nick did when he got up was turn on the percolator. He'd had no company last night, she had heard him come in alone, so she wouldn't be embarrassing anybody.

She walked into the kitchen from the top of the steps, through the open door, and from the living room she heard Peter say, 'What the hell am I going to do?'

'You'd better tell her.' Nick's voice was rough but recognisable.

'Tell her how? I meant to last night, but when she looks at you with those eyes of hers you feel such a swine. She's a super girl. She's so straight, so trusting. Only I'm just not ready to settle down, and that's what Sophy wants, isn't it? A home, you know, a mortgage, the lot.'

'What's wrong with that?' Nick demanded.

'Nothing,' said Peter. 'But you're not rushing into marriage, are you? You've got a nice place here and a steadier job than I've got, but I don't see you putting it about that you're looking for a wife.'

'In good time,' said Nick, who was still dating a different girl every other week. 'I want to be sure before——'

'Exactly!' Peter pounced on that, and Sophy clapped a hand to her mouth so that if she started to whimper it would be muffled. 'But I'm not sure. I'm sure that I'm crazy about her now, she's got something all right, but she's sure as hell not the smartest girl in the world, and in ten years' time—well, face it, how shall we be in ten years' time? And where? I want to get somewhere, and I don't think I can take Sophy along.'

He read the article, she thought. Of course he did. And Cress wasn't the only one who recognised me as the kind of girl who could only be a liability to a man.

She looked across at the sink and wondered if she could reach it before being sick, or whether she should rush down the steps and heave her heart out on the lawn. Whatever she did they mustn't hear her. She couldn't face either her brother or the man she had considered her lover. She couldn't face anyone, and she stumbled away on bare feet, down the steps and across the grass, into the house and up to her room.

Dry sobs were racking her, and her eyes burned as though they were filled with sand. She had felt so secure, so happy, so loved, but now she was more alone than she had ever been in her life.

On the wall, directly in front of her, hung a long-ago birthday present from her mother, a copy of an antique map of a mythical land peopled by legendary monsters. When Sophy was a child the dragons and the gorgons and the two-headed warriors had scared her in a delightful way because she had known that she was safe.

Sometimes she had imagined venturing into that perilous land with Peter at her side, protecting her. There would be no protection from Peter again, no love from him either, and yet she had to go on living, facing all the empty days and nights.

'Here be tygers,' read the script over the quaint little

sketch representing a jungle, and Sophy began to laugh as silently as she had sobbed. There were tigers all right. One tiger had savaged her life. She was not blaming Peter. Oddly she felt no bitterness against him, but a terrible anger was building up in her against the man called Tighe.

She would have liked to kill him. She was the girl who fed the birds and waited for the squirrel to come down and scamper about the lawn, but there was murder in her heart as she put on shoes and a green jacket that clashed with the pink dress she was wearing, without seeing or caring.

In the kitchen she left a note on the table, 'Gone out for the day, Sophy,' slipped her purse in her pocket and picked up the carrier bag with the sandwiches, and the cheese and apples, and the two cooked chicken joints. Peter's car was still in front of the house and she kept her eyes averted as she hurried past it. It hurt to even look at his car, she couldn't have faced Peter himself.

After a two-mile walk to the bus station she still had no clear idea what she planned to do, except get away for the day by the first bus available. She couldn't think why she was carrying the picnic, she certainly wouldn't be eating it, and she dropped the carrier bag into a refuse bin before she went into the station.

On Sunday morning most of the buses were heading for the coast and that would do well enough, she could lose herself in the crowds. Her eyes scanned the destination signs listlessly, and then she saw 'Buxham' go up on one of the buses and blinked at it, and frowned. Of *course*, Witherstone, near Buxham. The Old Mill House where there be tygers.

She wondered what the tiger was doing this morning. She was running away because of him. She would go back home tonight and try to carry on, but right now she was running, because she was one of the no-account dimwits he had warned all ambitious men against. A girl who listened and said nothing because she had nothing to say.

Well, this morning there was plenty she could have said. What right had he to sneer at quiet women? How did she know what went on in their heads?

I could tell him, she thought. I could say, 'Was that interview supposed to be funny? Well it wasn't. It wrecked my life and broke my heart, and what would a man like you know about love anyway?'

She got on the bus. The journey took almost an hour. Most of the time she looked out of the window, but she saw none of the scenery because in her mind she was in the panelled study, facing the tiger, because this morning she was a little crazy.

CHAPTER TWO

WHEN the bus finally drew up Sophy was still in a state of shock. She walked slowly out of the bus station into the town square, looking around but still hardly seeing anything. Most of the shops were closed. The main sign of activity was a crowd of youngsters, boys and girls wearing unisex gear of helmets, jeans and leather jackets, sitting astride stationary motorbikes discussing where they should make for today. Church bells were ringing somewhere, and as she passed Sophy got a wolf whistle from one of the leather-jacketed lads.

She didn't hear it. It was unlikely she would have heard if he had called her name. She was walking towards a taxi rank and the one taxi waiting there.

'Witherstone, please,' she said. 'Anywhere in the main road.'

It wasn't a village she knew well, but she did know it was on the edge of the moors, and perhaps she would walk over the moors. She liked walking although nothing would give her any pleasure today. The sun was shining still and there was hardly a cloud in the sky, and yet the world was black. She closed her eyes in the back of the taxi and when they slowed down and the driver asked, 'Will this do?' she said, 'Yes,' before she opened her eyes, so that he could have been putting her down anywhere.

It would do, wherever it was, and it was Witherstone, because it was on the sign over a post office-cum-general store. She paid the taxi, adding a tip, and he thanked her and wished her good morning, what was left in her purse wouldn't get her home. She was lucky it had got her here, she might not have had enough to pay him. As for getting back, she would hitch, or walk. Or phone, and somebody might fetch her. Not Peter, nor Nick, she couldn't travel back with them. They'd ask what she'd thought she was doing, and she couldn't say, 'I heard you talking.' Perhaps her mother or father might come, or Cress, but they would resent having to turn out to collect her and she would get no comfort.

She asked a woman, walking by with a small boy and a large dog, the way to the Old Mill House, and the directions were simple. The woman pointed out the road and Sophy nodded, 'Yes, I see—thank you,' and followed them, up and over a hill, and there were the gates, and behind, between the trees a big grey house.

The sun was so hot on the back of her head that she put up her hand as protection, and went through the open gates stumbling towards the house. Her head was swimming, and when she reached the door she hardly knew how she came to be there. The doorknocker was shaped like a ring of iron rope and she reached up and banged.

It was a nightmare, but now she was here, if she could get in and see him she would say, 'You don't know me, but this will only take a couple of minutes, so please listen. Everybody listens to you because you're a big man, a big success. Well, has it ever occurred to you that what you say could cause an awful lot of pain? I don't suppose it has, and I don't suppose you care, but that's why I'm here. To tell you you can smash up lives with words.'

Then she would walk out. Then she might feel better.

The heavy door swung open and Sophy was confronted by a harassed-looking woman, wearing a pink nylon overall and with her hair wisping around her face as though she had tried to pin it up and run out of hair pins.

'Please could I see Mr Tighe?' Sophy croaked. 'I——'

'Come in, miss.' The woman stood aside to let her through, closed the front door as Sophy stepped through, 'If you'd just wait in there.' She nodded towards an open door in the hall and hurried off down the corridor leaving her standing there.

Maybe the joint's burning, or the washer's overflowing, Sophy thought dully. Through the open door she could see panelled walls, and it was probably the study where he had given the interview. She moved towards it, her mouth dry and her steps jerky, half expecting to see the man behind the desk. But the room was empty, and that was a relief.

She shouldn't be here, asking to be insulted. 'Excuse me,' she would say, 'but I had a small nervous breakdown this morning and I think I'm just coming out of it. If you'd just let me out I'll start walking home.'

Long windows were open, framing a rustic scene of sun-dappled lawns and trees, and light dancing on water. Two children sat on the wall of a grey stone bridge, dark heads together, and as Sophy stood watching them one of them scrambled up on top of the wall and began to walk along wobbling precariously.

Sophy's heart leaped into her throat. This wasn't the little stream the reporter had mentioned, this was a lake, and it looked deep. 'Get down from there!' she called, as she started to run across the grass towards the lake, and the child threw up her arms and overbalanced, splashing in with a shriek. She didn't come up. When Sophy reached the water's edge there was no sign of the dark flowing curls. The second child, a boy, was emitting a high-pitched screech, all on one note. 'How deep is it?' Sophy yelled, and he stopped just long enough to say, 'Miles!' then took up the screech again as she tore off her jacket and kicked off her shoes, and dived from the centre of the bridge where the child had gone down.

It was clear sweet water but deep, with weeds among the pebbles on the bed, and she swam around under water searching with frantic eyes. The child should have come up, swimming or floundering, unless she was trapped in some way, and Sophy stayed down until her own lungs were almost bursting before she bobbed up to gulp in more air.

Both children were on the bridge, staring down. 'I—g-got out,' the girl hiccuped, and Sophy grinned back from sheer relief, swimming until she could touch bottom. The whole thing could only have taken a minute or two and the woman who had opened the door to her was racing across the grass, her hair looking even wilder, with Gavin Tighe just ahead.

The children shot off the bridge and ran, giving the man a wide berth. They're afraid of him, thought Sophy. It was an accident, that child was in danger, but she isn't running to him. They weren't running to the woman either, although they had ducked behind her into the house. Gavin Tighe slackened his pace and the woman reached Sophy, grabbing her as she emerged from the lake babbling, 'Are you all right? Oh, I don't know! Come on in.'

The children were in the kitchen when Sophy was ushered in, and the woman scolded shrilly, 'Get upstairs with you, and you keep out of his way!' Her tone changed. 'If you'd come this way, miss.' Both children vanished like lightning, the girl left a wet trail along the flagstones in the hall and Sophy went the same way, water dripping from her.

'In here,' said the woman, which was a bathroom near the top of the stairs. 'There's a robe behind the door, and if you'll put your things outside I'll get them washed and dried.' She was practically wringing her hands. 'I'm that sorry. The young limbs!'

'It was an accident,' said Sophy. And partly her fault because she had shouted and startled the child, who might otherwise have wobbled her way along the top of the wall without falling off it.

She turned on the taps and stripped off her clothes. The cold dip had cleared her head and let some common sense back in. She could hardly have felt more wretched, but at least now she knew what she was doing, having a hot bath and then getting herself warm and dry. She dropped her clothes on the floor outside the door and sat on the side of the bath, letting the steam curl around her and watching the water rising higher.

They were very beautiful children. The faces that had peered down from the bridge had been like two Jumeau dolls, round and rosy, with huge eyes fringed with extravagantly long lashes, the boy with dark crisp curls and the girl's wet hair longer but with the same curl and texture. Sophy could see them still, although her glimpse of them had been brief, and afterwards they had mostly been ducking and running.

She wondered whose children they were. They didn't look like the woman, who was old enough to be their grandmother, but they were obviously scared of Gavin Tighe. He and they had the same kind of hair, but at no time could he have had a cute little nose and a rosebud mouth. He had never looked like a Victorian doll, so maybe their mother had. He was a bachelor now, but he could have been talking about an ex-wife when he was ranting on about clinging women. If he was, poor woman. Poor kids, if he was their father.

She reached for a bottle that looked like bath oil, and moist from the condensation that was rapidly filling the bathroom, it slipped through her fingers and crashed on the tiled floor. Typical, she thought, I never lose my touch. She hadn't realised that her hands were shaking so badly that she had hardly any grip. But now as she gingerly picked up the glass shards and deposited them on a tissue she looked down at her trembling fingers, physical proof of the strain that the morning had been. She must steady herself. Everything was hellish, but she mustn't go to pieces. She would get out of here as soon as she could, and she would have to think of some explanation why she had asked to see Gavin Tighe that wasn't the truth because the truth sounded crazy.

This wasn't bath essence after all. It was aftershave lotion, and both the container and the smell seemed expensive. The bathroom reeked of it, and it was the first breakage that didn't worry her a whit. Let him buy himself another, she thought, he can afford it. She had been saved from making herself ridiculous, trying to tell him what she thought about him, but her opinion hadn't changed. If anything she disliked him even more, remembering how those children had shrunk away, and the woman saying, 'You keep out of his sight!'

She had only stayed in the bath long enough to wash away the clamminess of the lake from her skin and hair, then she jumped out and towelled herself dry. Her freshly permed hair was frizzled into a halo, Annie's pretty style obviously needed Annie's touch, and she was sitting on a stool rubbing her hair when there was a tap on the door and the woman called, 'All right, miss?'

'Fine.' Sophy grabbed the robe from behind the door and pulled it on hastily, then she opened the door. 'How's the little girl?'

'She'll live.' That was said with a touch of grimness, and the woman's nose twitched slightly as the concentrated aroma of aftershave came billowing out.

'I'm sorry,' said Sophy, 'but I broke a bottle.'

'That's all right, don't you bother, I'll see to it.' She seemed anxious to be reassuring and helpful. 'You drink this,' she said. 'I've got your clothes drying out. Oh, and Mr Tighe is in the study, he'd like to see you as soon as you're ready, because he's got to get off.'

'Tell him not to hang around for me,' said Sophy, 'because it doesn't matter at all.'

'Oh, you must see him!' Now the woman sounded so distressed that Sophy wondered if she could be scared of Gavin Tighe too, if he bullied the whole household. It wouldn't have surprised Sophy, she could easily imagine him as a domestic tyrant—and this was the man Peter envied! Nobody seemed very happy around here, that was for sure, and she couldn't think what she was going to say to him except that he made her sick and she just wanted to get out of his house.

She was clutching a glass of hot whisky that the woman had thrust into her hand, and she sat down again on the bathroom stool and sipped it slowly. She had never drunk whisky at this time in the day in her life, but then she had never dived into a lake fully dressed before and if she had to face Gavin Tighe she could use a little dutch courage. She could also have used her clothes, although this robe covered her adequately.

It was probably a woman's, a kimono in heavy cream silk with a huge scarlet peony embroidered on the back, and Cress would have looked fantastic in it. It wasn't Sophy's style, but she tied the girdle firmly round her waist, drained the whisky glass, and stood up, taking a deep breath. She wasn't going to tell anybody in this house her name even, much less where she came from and why she was here. She would say something like, 'I'm looking for a lost dog, I wondered if it had come into your garden,' and go into no further details. But what she would say was that it was criminal to let small children play near deep water, even if they could swim. It probably wasn't the first time they had done that balancing act along the wall, and it was so dangerous.

The whisky went straight to her head, which was all to the good. The study door was still ajar, and she peered round it and he was sitting at the desk. He stood up when he saw her and he was even taller than she remembered, so that she found herself standing straighter herself, stretching her neck and lifting her chin, although usually she slouched a little, trying to make herself smaller and less conspicuous.

'Are you all right?' he was asking her.

'Yes. How about——?'

'Felicity? Don't worry about her.' He sounded much as the woman had done, and Sophy said heatedly,

'Somebody should be worrying about them! She could have drowned in that lake!'

'They wouldn't drown in a whirlpool,' he said. 'They're amphibious.'

She couldn't believe that anyone could be so callous. 'Sit down, please,' he said, sitting down again himself, and now the whisky was reaching her knees, so she did sit in the nearest chair.

'How old are you? You only look a child yourself.'

Sophy said, 'Nearly twenty,' and she would have added, 'Why?' but he was asking her, 'Have you had any experience looking after children?' and then the phone rang and he said, 'Excuse me,' and picked it up.

It was a business call. He was talking what might as well have been a foreign language to her, and anyway she wasn't listening, she was weighing the implications of his questions. Why should he want to know if she had been in charge of children? And of course he didn't. Not if Sophy Wade had, so he must be mistaking her for somebody else. Somebody must be coming here about a job. As what? Teacher? Nanny? The genuine article could be walking in any minute, but it did offer Sophy a chance to get out of the house without racking her brain for a reason why she was here. She must get the interview over and get out as soon as her clothes were dry.

'Right, you do that,' he said, and put down the phone and turned his eyes on Sophy. 'Well? Have you?'

'What?' His eyes were as dark as the children's, but there was nothing wistful about them. They bored like laser beams.

'What experience have you had, looking after children?' He was repeating himself with a patience that she expected to short-circuit any minute, and she said,

'I've looked after friends' children.'

'You like children?'

'Yes.' Some folk didn't, of course. He didn't. He couldn't, or they wouldn't run from him, and she hoped this nanny he was hiring would stand up for them and give them affection and security.

'You understand it's a temporary job? They're home from boarding school for the Easter holidays, which have started early this year because of an epidemic of chickenpox. Have you had chickenpox?'

'Yes.'

'So have they, so there should be no trouble, although they told one young woman they were

covered with spots under their jeans. She decided not
to bother with the job.'

Sophy's lips twitched. 'I don't blame her. Why did
they tell her that?'

'They don't want a nanny.'

She wasn't wanted at home, and now she had
walked into an interview to become an unwanted
nanny—that had its funny side, she supposed. 'Well,
they need one,' she said, 'if it's only to keep them off
that wall. They're a bit young to be at boarding
school, aren't they? How old are they?'

'Seven.'

'Twins, then. And how long have they been away at
school?' She was questioning *him*, and it was the
whisky that was giving her the courage, but she could
feel an affinity for any unwanted child.

'Since they were five.' She wondered again about
their mother, but she daren't ask. 'You have
references?' he wanted to know, and she heard herself
say,

'I can bring them.' From the vicar. The bank
manager. Or their local M.P. Her parents' friends. She
was being considered for the job and if it was offered
she was going to take it, because here was a chance to
get away from home for a few weeks and away from
Peter. No one had imagined that Sophy might ever
strike out on her own. It would be a little triumph to
go back tonight and tell them she was starting work
tomorrow.

'Do you drive?' he was asking her.

'I have a licence.' There was a difference, but she
was legally entitled to sit behind a wheel.

There was a tap on the door and the woman looked
in and Gavin Tighe got to his feet. 'I'm on my way,
Mrs Greenhaugh, thank you. Perhaps you would settle
things with Miss—er——' He smiled a brief smile at

Sophy and strode out of the room, and the woman came in and said hopefully, 'Can you start right away?'

'Tomorrow,' said Sophy, wondering whether she should confess that she was here by coincidence, and she hadn't known there was a job going, when the woman said,

'Would you be from the agency?'

'No.'

'You saw the advert, then? I wrote the names down when they phoned, but I don't know where the list's got to. Your name's——' She waited and Sophy told her, then asked before Mrs Greenhaugh had time to ponder, 'Have you had many applicants?'

'There's been no rush when they heard where we were.' Witherstone was a small village. It would not offer much in the way of off-duty entertainment, although Sophy would have thought that having Gavin Tighe about the house might appeal to some women. She probably had been offered the post because she had dived into the lake so promptly, proving herself a good watchdog.

'I've got your clothes drying,' said Mrs Greenhaugh.

'Thank you.' Sophy looked down at her bare feet. 'I left my shoes and my jacket outside.'

'They're in the kitchen. Shall we go along to my room and have a cup of tea?'

'That would be lovely,' said Sophy gratefully. 'I'm not really used to whisky.' Mrs Greenhaugh stood looking hard at her for a moment, then she aked. 'How old are you?' She didn't add, as he had, 'You don't look much more than a child yourself,' but Sophy presumed that was what she was thinking, and she supposed she must look like a well-scrubbed child. About the face anyway.

'Nineteen,' she said. Twenty in three months' time,

but 'nearly twenty' had sounded older, and she had
objected to Gavin Tighe considering her a child.

'Well, I hope you can manage them,' said Mrs
Greenhaugh. 'Don't you let them get the upper hand.'

She led the way down the hall and Sophy followed
close behind. This day had sprung so many surprises
that her mind was reeling. She wouldn't think about
Peter. She would just concentrate on this house and
what was happening to her here. That was enough for
the present.

The room was cluttered and cosy. There were
chintz-covered armchairs and china ornaments and a
round table with a bobbled tablecloth. Through an
open door leading into the kitchen, Sophy saw her
clothes airing on a clothes horse in front of an Aga
stove. Her bra and pants looked ridiculously conspicuous and she found herself blushing like an idiot,
conscious of her nakedness beneath the robe.

She nearly jumped up and dashed into the kitchen
and grabbed her undies, but the robe covered her from
head to foot, for goodness' sake, and although Mrs
Greenhaugh was obviously glad to get a nanny she had
reservations about Sophy. A little poise and decorum
were called for, so Sophy sat still and looked at the
row of Staffordshire dogs on the mantelpiece, until
Mrs Greenhaugh brought in a tray from the kitchen,
with teacups and a pot under a patchwork cosy.
'Now,' said Mrs Greenhaugh, sitting down and
getting down to business, 'what were you expecting in
the way of wages?'

'What are you offering?' asked Sophy, who had no
idea of the market price of an untrained nanny. When
Mrs Greenhaugh gave a figure it sounded rather a lot,
and she nodded.

'You'll start tomorrow?' Sophy nodded again.
'Weekends off or double time if you stay.' She would

probably stay. She needed to get right away from home for a while. 'They're due back at school in five weeks' time,' Mrs Greenhaugh went on, and Sophy thought, if I can hold down this job I will have had experience, then I could go to an agency and see about another post.

She said, 'I'd like to come here very much,' and Mrs Greenhaugh began to pour out a cup of tea and said, 'Well, I hope you'll be happy here, but——' She paused, frowned at the teapot, then asked if Sophy took sugar, and Sophy felt she could have added the missing words herself, 'but he isn't an easy man to work for.'

While they drank their tea she answered Mrs Greenhaugh's questions about her family, and it all sounded very reassuring and respectable. She didn't say that she had never measured up to her parents' standards, that Cressida was all the daughters they had needed. But when she had told Mrs Greenhaugh about her mother's antique shop she did ask, 'What about the children's mother? Where is she?'

'Dead, poor young thing,' Mrs Greenhaugh's face shadowed. So the children were motherless, and pity filled Sophy for them. She put down her empty cup and said, 'If I could get into my clothes now perhaps I could see them.'

'You'd like to see your room as well, wouldn't you?' Mrs Greenhaugh got up. 'You can change in there, and the children are in the nursery.'

The room that was to be Sophy's was pleasant and light, with a window overlooking the garden. Beyond that the hills of the moors stretched away into the distance. She would be sleeping here tomorrow night, starting a new life that might not make her happy but where at last she would be useful and needed. The children needed her, she was convinced of that, and she needed them to fill the void in her heart and her life. Hearing Peter and Nick talking this morning had been like falling into a black pit.

There were mirrors around—an oval one over a rosewood dressing table, a full-length one behind the door of a wardrobe. When Sophy was dressed in her own clothes again she saw herself, and it was a depressing sight. The dip in the lake, and then the speedy wash and dry, had done nothing for the pink cotton dress, and without even a touch of make-up or a comb for her hair Sophy looked washed out herself.

She opened the door that led to the nursery and the two children looked up from two books set before them. 'Please,' said Sophy, 'could somebody lend me a comb?'

The girl went into another room and came out holding a comb which she handed over, her lips curling very slightly in answer to Sophy's smile. 'Thank you,' said Sophy, dragging the comb through her hair and wincing at the tangles. 'I'm Sophy.'

'I'm Felicity,' said the girl, 'and this is Charles.' The boy said nothing. 'I'm sorry I got you wet,' said the girl, 'I swim quite well, you know.'

Sophy laughed, 'Now I know. Your father told me,' and the girl's eyes flew wide open.

'Our father? He's not our father!'

Oh no, thought Sophy, what have I said? 'He's our uncle,' said the boy. 'We're orphans.'

They looked heartbreaking, and she felt tears welling in her eyes and wondered whether they were for the children or herself. Gavin Tighe was a hard man and the world was a lonely place. 'Is he——' she had to ask this, 'Is he kind to you?' and the two pale set little faces should have answered her, but Charles said,

'He doesn't like us coming here much. When he's here he tells us to be quiet.'

Surely this place was big enough for children to let off steam without disturbing anybody. If it wasn't the garden was, and then there were the moors.

'We don't like holidays much,' said Felicity. 'We'd rather be at school.'

That was awful. 'This holiday is going to be different,' Sophy promised.

'How?' they chorused in unison, both watching her with big eyes.

'Because I'll be here. We'll think of things to do.' They had been reading quietly when she came into the room, but seven-year-old children on holiday on a lovely day should have been running and playing. 'It's lovely here,' she said. 'The moors are just over the wall where we can keep out of everyone's way and have a super time.'

'Now?' Again they both spoke together, this time with eagerness, and their eyes brightened. A walk would help her to get to know them before she started thinking about getting home.

'Why not?' she smiled. 'I'll go and ask Mrs Greenhaugh if it's all right. I'll be right back.'

There was a man in the kitchen when Sophy walked in. He had just brought in vegetables that Mrs Greenhaugh was emptying out of a skip. Spring greens, and tiny new potatoes, earth-covered.

'This is Tom,' said Mrs Greenhaugh. 'I was just telling him about you.'

Tom looked at Sophy from under grizzled eyebrows and she thought, I bet I know what you were saying; because from his expression he was wondering how Sophy was going to fit in here. She did look vulnerable, she always had. She looked as though she would scare easily and be easily hurt, but nothing was likely to hurt her again as badly as losing Peter. Certainly nothing Gavin Tighe could do or say. Don't

worry about me, she could have told them, I'm
fireproof.

She said hello to Tom, and then asked, 'Could I
take the children for a walk? It's such a lovely day.'

Neither answered at once. They exchanged glances,
then Tom said, 'Aye, all right, but you keep an eye on
them, they're a pair of young rips.'

'I will.' They had probably run over his vegetables
or his flower beds. Gardeners were notoriously touchy
about things like that. She said, 'I didn't realise Mr
Tighe was their uncle, I thought he was their father.'

'They're his sister's children,' said Mrs Greenhaugh.
'Her husband was piloting the plane.' She shook her
head and sighed, and Sophy said,

'They told me they were orphans. How terrible for
them!'

'They've got a lot to be thankful for,' Tom said
gruffly. 'Better off than most children, they are,' and
Sophy didn't argue, although she disagreed. In
material things the twins might be well off, but what
substitute was Gavin Tighe for loving parents?

There was a heavy old door in the garden wall that
led on to the moors, and it was quite magical pulling
back the bolt at the top, lifting the latch and swinging
the door open. It made Sophy think of the Enchanted
Garden, the tended lawns and the landscaped lake
behind them, the house overlooking all, and ahead the
wildness of the moors. The children shot through,
squealing with delight, arms flailing like wings as
though they would take off any minute; and Sophy
stood for a few seconds in the gateway. Then the
feeling of being freed got her too, and she was
laughing and running with them.

They went skimming over the rough grass, leaping
ditches and lighting on hillocks. And Sophy ran, so
that she had no time to think about Peter, with the sun

on her face and wind in her hair. Briars tore her tights, and the children caught her hand, sometimes both hands, and took her to see the Seven Springs and the Hanging Oak.

It took longer to get back. She shouldn't have let them come so far, overtiring themselves, because the moment she said, 'We must go home now,' and turned round they sagged.

'Do you know the way?' asked Felicity, and Sophy said,

'Of course. I just go back the way I came, don't I?' She was almost sure she could remember landmarks, but she wasn't admitting she was in their hands, although she didn't think for a minute that they were going to pretend to be lost.

Of course they didn't. They went back, but slowly, dragging their feet. They were too heavy to carry. She tried piggybacks until they brought her down to her knees. After that she had to let them sit and rest several times, and when they came to a strange-shaped rock that she recognised as being not too far from the house she was profoundly relieved. They had insisted they were taking her a short cut back, that was why they hadn't passed Seven Springs again, and she had to accept that because she didn't know the way herself. But all in all this walk had taken much longer than she'd planned, and she hoped they weren't worrying about the children back at the house.

She also hoped that Gavin Tighe was out for the day, but that hope was dashed when she saw him striding over the moor towards them. The twins had seen him too. Felicity gave a nervous little skip, and then they both moved together and waited by Sophy's side.

'Where the hell have you been?' he demanded, reaching them. 'Do you know what time it is?'

'Well, no, not actually. I haven't got a watch on. I know we've been out longer than I meant to be, we've been on a long walk, the children must be ravenous.' He was making her babble.

'Go on,' he said to them and they darted past him, running as fast as they had when they first came out here. Sophy, with her torn tights and her hair in an even wilder tangle, was uncomfortably aware of her own sorry state.

'Sorry,' she said.

'Do you know these moors?' He asked the question, frowning down at her, and then started back for the house with long strides. She walked beside him, answering,

'I've been here before, but I don't know them well.'

'Then don't you think it might have been wiser to have kept the house in sight?'

'I suppose so.' Now she could admit to herself that she had begun to wonder what she would do if night fell and she hadn't got the children back. It had been like letting two untrained puppies off the leash, or two birds out of a cage.

'Miss Wade,' said Gavin Tighe, 'I'm not sure that you're right for this job.'

But she was. She was meant for it. The way things had happened this morning had to be fate taking a hand. 'Oh, I *am*!' she said earnestly.

'I'm not sure you can control the children.' When he said 'control' it sounded grim. She stole a look at him as they walked side by side and thought he had the hardest mouth and chin she had ever seen. She was sure he was a strict disciplinarian, no wonder the twins didn't want to go back to the house. They preferred the moors, and who wouldn't?

'Please,' she said, 'let me try.'

They were approaching the gate in the wall and she

was beginning to think he wasn't discussing it any further, but as they skirted the lake he said, 'Well, we certainly owe you something, so we'll settle for a week's trial.'

'Thank you.'

'You'd better get something to eat and then Tom will run you home. You didn't come in a car, did you?'

'No.' She would be glad of the lift. She could hardly have asked for a fiver on account.

'Until tomorrow, then,' he said, but he would surely be working tomorrow and with any luck at all she would keep herself, and the children, out of his way. He made her uncomfortable, and it wasn't just the usual shyness she felt with strangers. 'By the pricking of my thumbs something wicked this way comes,' said Shakespeare's witch, but in Sophy's case, with this man, the pricking seemed to run the whole length of her spine, jarring her whole nervous system.

The children were eating in the nursery, Sophy offered to take up their tray, but Mrs Greenhaugh said, 'You sit down. You've done enough running around after them for one day.' She seemed a kind enough woman, but with a house this size to run Sophy could understand that two small and active children might get on her nerves. She said, 'It wasn't their fault we were out so long, I lost count of the time, it's such a beautiful spring day.'

Spring should be a beginning, but for Sophy today had been an ending. Oh, Peter! she thought, as the pain came flooding back, and she sat down, and Mrs Greenhaugh said, 'You look worn out. I don't think you're going to——'

'I'm fine,' said Sophy quickly, and made herself smile.

She wasn't hungry herself, not even after all that strong fresh air. The food went dry in her mouth and stuck in her throat but she chewed and swallowed doggedly, getting it down, because she had to go back home now and she would need strength for that. It was too much to hope that the family would take her announcement that she had found herself a job and was leaving tomorrow without asking a lot of questions. And how was she going to face Peter, pretending she still had no idea that last night when she had worried because he looked haggard, he was trying to find the courage to dump her?

Well, she had the journey home to compose herself, and rehearse her lines. She didn't think Tom would be chatting. He seemed a dour old Yorkshireman.

She was washing her plate at the kitchen sink when Gavin Tighe walked in and asked, 'Are you ready?'

'To go? Yes. See you tomorrow, Mrs Greenhaugh.' She grabbed the jacket she had hung on a hook in the kitchen when she came back into the house, and hurried down the hall after him.

He went through the front door and she followed. A car was waiting, a black Mercedes, but nobody was in the driver's seat. He opened the passenger door, left it swinging and went round to get behind the wheel himself, and Sophy gasped, making no attempt to get in, 'Where's—er—Tom?'

'Out,' said Gavin Tighe. 'I'll take you.'

She did not want him to drive her anywhere. He might ask questions on the way, and discover she hadn't seen an advertisement. He might begin to suspect how much she disliked him. If she had to sit by him for up to thirty minutes she wasn't going to be able to cope with anything at the other end, she was going to be a nervous wreck.

'Your reflexes seem to have slowed down since this morning,' he drawled, and she couldn't say that she wouldn't dream of troubling him because she didn't have enough money for a taxi and a bus. She had to get in beside him, and she did.

He didn't start up the car immediately. He sat, looking at her, the frown line between his dark brows. 'Bring your references tomorrow,' he said.

'What?' She'd heard him and she could get them, but he made her stammer. 'Oh yes, I will,' she said.

He started the engine then and the car moved smoothly away, and Sophy knew that he was regretting even that week's trial and that, on any excuse at all, he would dump her too.

CHAPTER THREE

'WHAT'S your address?' Gavin Tighe asked Sophy as the car reached the end of the drive, and she wondered what he would have said if she'd said 'Brighton'. Although Mrs Greenhaugh had probably told him she was a Northern girl. After she answered his question there was no more talk, and she was grateful for that. He would only have to ask, 'What paper did you see the advertisement in?' for her to be in real trouble.

She tried to shut him out and work out what she was going to say when she got home, but that was impossible. He had the kind of presence that had made her feel shut in when he'd walked beside her on the moors. In the cabin of a car he was overwhelming, so that all she could do was sit with her fingers laced tight, longing for the journey to end.

She pushed back her hair when a lock fell into her eyes and was convinced that the aroma of that aftershave still lingered on her fingers. Of course it could be him, and she had a vision of him slapping it on in the bathroom on wet hard skin. Well, he wouldn't tomorrow, and she wondered if when she arrived at his home in the morning he would say, 'Sorry, Miss Wade, but someone as clumsy as you has to be a hazard around the house.'

She was sure he had shut her out completely, that so far as he was concerned he was travelling alone, and she surely wouldn't want to be his travelling companion. All she wanted was to get where she was going and get out of the car.

'You'll have to direct me from here,' he said, as they approached the outskirts of her home town, and she had to cough to clear her throat before she could even manage to do that. Sophy's suburb was through the town centre and past her mother's antique shop which stood on a corner, by traffic lights. They were held up for a few moments until the lights changed to green, but she didn't point out the shop. There was a doll in the window, and she didn't say, 'Do you know that the twins look like Jumeau dolls in jeans and T-shirts Mr Tighe? No, of course you don't.'

If his car drew up outside her house it was possible someone would see it and come out. She would have to introduce them, and she couldn't handle the confusion that would cause. So when they reached the end of her road she said, 'Would you put me down here, please? This is where I want to get out.'

He stopped at once, and she scrambled out as he said, 'We'll see you in the morning.'

'Yes, thank you for the lift.' The car drove away and she waited until it came back, having turned in the first side street. Gavin Tighe raised a hand in signal as he passed her and Sophy managed a jerky little answering wave. He hadn't wanted to see her home nor her family. He didn't expect to be saddled with her for even the five weeks of the school holidays, but she had to hold on to this job. She had to prove herself in some way, she couldn't bear to be rejected again.

Dusk was beginning to fall. The evening air was growing chilly, and Sophy shivered walking along the street. There were no cars in the drive. The double garage doors were closed and there was no sign of activity. The Wade home was a well-built detached Edwardian which was always bandbox neat because neither of Sophy's parents could bear untidiness, the curtains at the windows hung in their pleated folds, with a light on here and there, but nobody was looking out for Sophy.

Maybe they haven't missed me, she thought crazily. Maybe nobody saw the note and nobody noticed I wasn't there. They all thought I was in another room and nobody bothered to look.

She opened the front door and walked into the hall as her mother was crossing it. '*Sophy!*' exclaimed her mother. 'Where on *earth* have you been?' She raised her voice. 'Gilbert, she's back!'

'Of course she's back,' Sophy's father replied wearily from the drawing room. So there had been a small fuss, and he hated disturbances.

'Where *have* you been?' her mother was asking her again, testily as though Sophy had been tiresome, and while Sophy was still wondering how to start explaining, 'Did you mention you'd be out today?'

Sara Wade wasn't sure about that, she never paid much attention to what her younger daughter was saying, and Sophy gave a little shrug and her mother said, 'I thought you might have done, but I couldn't remember where you said you were going. Peter's been very bothered.' Sara had been astonished at how bothered Peter had been when he heard that Sophy had taken herself off. He had acted as though it was something unheard of, although of course it wasn't. The child had friends. 'He and Nick have been ringing around,' Sara went on, 'and they've been out looking for you.'

'Oh dear,' said Sophy, thinking of the open door into Nick's flat and her habit of popping up there at weekends for a first cup of coffee. The men must have looked at each other when that note was found on the kitchen table, wondering if Sophy had overheard their conversation.

She followed her mother into the drawing room.

There was a discussion programme on the television which was getting all her father's attention, he didn't even look away from the screen when Sophy went in. Her mother sat down and picked up the *Sunday Telegraph* colour supplement.

'I went after a job,' said Sophy, and they both looked at her then.

'You *what*?' exclaimed her mother.

'What kind of job?' her father asked.

'A temporary one. Looking after twins of seven on holiday from boarding school.' If she mentioned Gavin Tighe the questions would never stop. 'For a Mrs Greenhaugh,' she said, 'of Witherstone. Who seems very nice and so do the children.'

'You got the job?' Her mother was interested enough to ask that.

'Yes,' she said. 'I start tomorrow, and I have to take references.'

Her mother's dark beautiful brows rose and her voice chilled. 'I should have thought your family was reference enough!'

'Well, Mrs Greenhaugh doesn't know you, does she?' Sophy pointed out. The Wades were somebodies in this town, but she didn't think Gavin Tighe had ever heard of them. She said, 'I thought the vicar wouldn't mind saying I'm honest and healthy.'

Nobody smiled, and her father said, 'Phone Cress and tell her you're home,' as he turned back to the television. Cressida was the apple of his eye. If Peter and Nick had alarmed Cress about Sophy's safety her father would want her reassured at once.

'I will,' promised Sophy, and went to the phone in the hall and tried to ring her sister.

There was no reply, so Cress and Rob were not at home, and Sophy knew they wouldn't be searching for her. They'd be visiting friends, having a meal out, something like that, and she had to get these references to take with her tomorrow, so she must waste no more time.

She rang three prominent locals, who had known her from a child and who all said of course they would be delighted to give her a character reference. Sophy said she would be round in an hour or so to collect, if that was all right, and she was packing when Nick walked into her bedroom. He smiled but watched her keenly as he asked, 'What's all this, about you going after a job?' and she beamed back at him,

'And getting it, that's the thing.'

'Bit sudden, wasn't it?'

'Not that sudden.' She had a big case open on her bed into which she was packing most of her wardrobe, because she didn't want to come back here, not even for weekends, for at least a month. She folded a dress and laid it on top and told her brother, 'You don't just walk into jobs these days, unless it's with friends. I saw the advert last week and phoned for an interview right away.'

'Why didn't you mention it?' He had always considered Sophy an open book. He had never imagined her having secrets.

'Because I thought I wouldn't get it,' she said promptly, and he could understand that. 'The money's good.' When she told him what they would be paying her, 'And of course board and lodgings,' he nodded, almost impressed.

'Not bad. Yes, you're a dark horse, aren't you?' He had been worried about her all day, even though their mother had thought she remembered Sophy saying she was going somewhere. Nick was fond of Sophy, and now Peter was cooling off it would be easier if she found another interest that took her away for a while.

'I must phone Peter,' she said, and she was surprised how bright that sounded.

Nick said, 'I rang him. He's coming round.'

'That's nice.' Sophy went on smiling until her brother was reassured. With all his legal training and his sharp mind she was fooling him. She would never have thought she could do that. She had never wanted to do that before. When Peter came round to say goodbye she had to fool him too. She said, 'Would you give me a lift? I've got to collect a couple of references, unless you'd like to lend your car.'

Sophy's driving was another family joke. She had taken lessons at a driving school, the family didn't have time to teach her, and everyone agreed it had to be a fluke when she passed her test first time. Nick had let her do one run in his car, but she clipped the gate coming back, so that was it; and her mother had let her chauffeur until she decided that sitting by Sophy was more exhausting than negotiating the traffic herself.

'Sure I'll take you,' said Nick, 'and how are you going to get there in the morning? I've got an appointment at ten, but I'll run you to Witherstone if you like.' He was not usually so considerate, but right now he was relieved and knew that Sophy had lost Peter and he was feeling sorry for her.

They collected the three references, which were handed over with good wishes, and she read them out to Nick as they drove back home. They were very complimentary and he grinned, 'It is only a couple of kids you're in charge of, isn't it? What's the woman want all this for?'

'I don't know,' said Sophy. 'But I was told to bring some references.'

'You can take me,' said Nick, 'and I'll ask for her references if you're moving into her house.'

Sophy refolded the page she had been reading and slipped it back in the envelope and said, 'I've been thinking, and I don't want you bothering tomorrow. I shall catch a bus to Buxham, then get a taxi, and it will be no trouble at all. In fact I think I'd rather go on my own.'

'Please yourself,' said her brother cheerfully.

Peter's car was there when they got home and Sophy felt faint, because she did love him. These last two months they had spent so much time together that he would surely miss her when he was away, even though she had heard him telling Nick that if he meant to get somewhere in his life he couldn't take Sophy along. But he had also said she sure as hell wasn't the smartest girl alive, but she'd got something all right. When he saw she wasn't out to trap him into immediate marriage he might feel differently about her.

He was in the drawing room with her parents, standing as though he had jumped up from his chair when he'd heard the car drive up but couldn't decide whether to come to meet them or not. He looked for Nick behind her, and Nick shook his head very slightly with an expression that said, 'Nothing to do with that. She didn't hear what we were saying. Hold it for now.' All in a flash. Sophy saw her brother's reflection in the long Italian mirror and saw Peter's face clear and knew that both men cared for her, neither wanted her hurt.

Peter asked, 'What's all this about you going away? What are they like, the couple you'll be working for?'

'Seven years old,' she said, wilfully misunderstanding. 'And very beautiful. Like two Jumeau dolls.'

'Good heavens!' said her mother faintly.

'I meant your employers,' Peter persisted, and she said,

'Very nice.' She wondered how Peter would react if she confessed, 'Actually Mrs Greenhaugh is the housekeeper. My boss will be Gavin Tighe.' She wouldn't say that, but she could smell that aftershave again and it was almost as though Gavin Tighe had come into the room. She thought, Peter, I know you're clever and ambitious, and I don't know what it is about him, and I dislike him very much, but I know that if he did walk into this room he would dwarf you all.

She began to say her piece, about seeing the advertisement and fixing an interview; what the village was like, what the house was like, the children's names. There was a housekeeper and a gardener on the staff, maybe others, but those were all she had seen.

'Who's going to do my typing?' her father demanded, and Sophy hesitated in the middle of a sentence and her mother said,

'Cress will. It will only be for a few weeks,' and Gilbert Wade nodded, mollified.

The garden might be a problem, they hadn't thought of that yet, but none of them could see any objection to Sophy going away. It sounded a nice little temporary job in which she should be happy. She wasn't needed here. She was tolerated and treated kindly, but she mattered deeply to none of them. Not even to Peter. Not after what she had overheard this morning.

'What time off do you get?' he wanted to know.

'Weekends if I want them.'

'Of course you'll want them.' That meant that if she came home he might come round, maybe take her out.

'Maybe,' she said, and waved the three envelopes she was carrying. 'I've been collecting references because they'd like some, and I had no idea I was such a desirable employee. I seem to have been undervaluing myself all these years!'

They all smiled then, including her father, but they were sure they knew Sophy's value which wouldn't be high on the open market. She was a good kind girl, but not over-bright.

'Well, you've sprung a surprise on us all,' said Nick, and Sophy smiled brightly and thought bitterly, 'I'm surprising myself, I never realised I was an actress before.'

She finished her packing and went to bed early. It would be an early start in the morning. Peter had kissed her goodbye and gone off with a light step, and she had stayed calm and apparently cheerful until she was in her room alone. Then she wept a little, because he had gone without looking back.

Tomorrow night she would be in a different bed, in a different house, and she lay for a moment or two with the light still on, looking across at the 'old' map of the mythical land where 'there be tygers'. From tomorrow she would be in the jungle with the tiger with no protector at all . . .

This time Sophy's taxi took her to the door of the Old Mill House, and she climbed out and paid the taxi driver at nine o'clock precisely. She hadn't seen her father before she left, but her mother ran her to the bus stop, and offered a cool cheek to kiss and reminded her that she had promised to phone. Sophy had left this phone number. If anyone rang her they would discover who her employer was, but there was nothing she could do about that and it didn't really matter. No one had asked for her new address.

The children came out of the front door, looking clean and tidy, still in jeans and T-shirts. 'Hello,' said Charles, 'have you come to stay?'

'Yes,' said Sophy, and they smiled slightly. It wasn't much of a welcome, but Charles offered to carry her case, so they were accepting her, and she was glad to see Tom following them. The case could have been too heavy for a slightly built seven-year-old, but Charles' pride might have been hurt if Sophy had pointed that out. As it was Tom picked up the case and said, 'Morning, miss,' leading the way into the house, and nodded towards the kitchen. 'The wife's in there.'

So his wife was Mrs Greenhaugh, and she was loading up a washer. She said hello and introduced Sophy to a thin woman called Agnes, and asked, 'Will you be all right for a bit, we're up to our eyes in here?'

'Of course,' said Sophy. She took the three envelopes containing her references out of her handbag and put them on the kitchen table and asked, 'If Mr Tighe's around would you please see he gets these? He asked me to bring them this morning, so perhaps he wants to see them as soon as possible.'

'As soon as he gets back tonight,' Mrs Greenhaugh promised.

Unpacking didn't take long. Sophy didn't have that many clothes. Cress was the one who 'paid for dressing' as a girl, and who had grown up with flair and a size eight figure. The twins stood in the doorway of her bedroom with the nursery behind them, watching her, as she hung up the row of rather shapeless garments, and she made an effort to snap out of her depression, tossing the odds and ends of undies and night attire into a drawer and then saying brightly, 'How about showing me around the house? Unless somebody shows me round I could get lost.'

It was a biggish house and it seemed rather forbidding to Sophy, perhaps because of all the closed doors that the twins were not allowed to open. 'We mustn't go in there,' Felicity told her. 'We mustn't go anywhere but our room upstairs.'

'And the bathroom,' said Charles.

'Oh well, yes, the bathroom,' agreed Felicity.

They walked the corridors, six or seven bedrooms, Sophy thought. With nooks and crannies and little winding staircases it was a rambling old place where children could have had a wonderful time if they had been allowed to roam around. As it was the conducted tour was soon over, and Charles asked, 'Can we go out now?'

Today was duller than yesterday. The garden would be fine, but she didn't feel like risking the moors again and she said, 'We'll stay near the house this morning.'

'He was angry yesterday,' said Felicity suddenly.

'Your uncle? Why?'

'Because we were away a long time. He said it was our fault.' Sophy was horrified to see the child's huge dark eyes brimming with tears, and one rolled down her cheek.

'It was my fault too,' she said, and held Felicity fiercely for a moment. 'Come on, let's go into the garden.'

They could explore there, and Sophy played with them, everything from tag to tree climbing. At first she was scared they might fall when they went clambering up and she did call, 'That's high enough!' and Charles called down, 'Can you climb?'

'I could.' It was a horse chestnut with thick strong boughs, a perfect climbing tree once you had swung yourself off the ground, and she went up after them because that was the surest way of keeping them from climbing too high.

She hadn't climbed a tree in years. Not since she was a child herself. That tree in the garden at home had once been her secret den, and the twins were sitting on a tangle of branches that had made a little platform, and she guessed that this was their hiding place. They reminded her of herself years ago, although she had never been so beautiful, and she was making sure they had a happy day.

She went into the kitchen to see about meals, and Mrs Greenhaugh said half past one. No, thank you, there was nothing Sophy could do, but as it was starting to rain didn't she think they had all better come inside? The rain was more like a mist and Sophy had already suggested going back into the house, but Felicity had said, 'It's nicer out here,' and under the shelter of the trees Sophy had started telling them a story.

She went back to say that Mrs Greenhaugh thought they should all be indoors, and after that it was the nursery. There was nothing wrong with the nursery. It was a big room, with a big table in the middle, chairs around, a chest of drawers and a huge locked cupboard. 'What's in the cupboard?' Sophy asked. 'Where's the key?'

'I broke a doll,' said Felicity sadly. 'The toys are put up.'

'For a week,' said Charles.

'It was an accident, wasn't it?' said Sophy. 'I'll have to ask about that.'

'Don't fuss,' said Charles. 'It's only till Wednesday.'

The punishment seemed harsh for an accident, but they were accepting it, and the rest of the day was spent in the nursery. There was paper and colouring pencils in one of the drawers, and they made pictures and told sad little stories around them. Sophy was perturbed because nothing happy seemed to happen to the children they created. They were either locked up or devoured by space invaders, and Sophy felt you wouldn't have to be a child psychologist to suspect the deep insecurity behind all this.

She started to plan. This was the school holidays

and Gavin Tighe did want them kept out of his way, so he surely couldn't object to her getting them out of the house. She could take them trips. There were lots of places they could go, and she made a list so that by bedtime they were chattering eagerly and, it seemed, happily.

They had their meals upstairs. Mrs Greenhaugh looked in several times to ask if Sophy was all right, and Sophy said she was, of course, and until the children were bathed and in bed she had been having quite a pleasant time.

Mrs Greenhaugh came up to the nursery again, about half past seven—bedtime was seven o'clock—to ask if Sophy wouldn't like to come down. 'Mr Gavin's not back yet,' Mrs Greenhaugh. 'If you want to see him about anything he'll be back later.' Sophy would have to get his permission about taking the children out, but she couldn't face him tonight. It had been a full day and she was tired. She said, 'Thank you, but I think I'll stay up here. I don't think there are any problems.'

'I'm glad to hear that,' said Mrs Greenhaugh.

The problem was Sophy herself, and she was very aware of it. When the children were sleeping all she had to do was tidy up and sit around, and then get ready for bed, facing her own loneliness. She was going to miss Peter terribly. She had loved him so long, and when it had seemed that all her dreams were coming true suddenly it was over. She was scared to go to bed because when she woke she might not remember it was over. She might wake thinking he loved her, and then the pain would come and she might start crying and never be able to stop.

Even the children's pictures seemed to have a nightmarish quality. She looked at them all again, one by one, seeing in these little running figures nothing but fear and loneliness, and when she had shut them in a drawer and she was huddled under the sheets she felt like a lonely child herself.

'Oh, Peter,' she whispered, 'Oh, Peter, Peter...' and his name echoed in her mind, down long corridors. His face came clearly and then dissolved, and she tossed and turned and fell at last into a disturbed sleep, stifling sobs, her face pressed into the pillow.

Some time during the night the old dream came back, where she was running with outstretched hands, searching but not knowing what she was looking for. In an empty town, in a swirling fog, peering through windows into empty rooms, down deserted streets with slithering stones beneath her feet. And then she was falling down a hill, banging her head on the stones, bumping, hurting until the sickening jarring moment when she woke and found herself in a crumpled heap in the darkness.

There was carpet beneath her. Her head was on a step. She had been *sleepwalking*, and nausea racked her so that she began to heave, pressing both hands over her mouth, huddling down against the rough carpet. Light came on brutally and she moaned. She was fully conscious now, she saw the man looming over her, but she couldn't stand yet. She had fallen down three, four steps, and she was shaking from the dream and the shock. She heard him ask, 'Are you ill?' and she shook her head. He was lifting her up, half carrying her as she stumbled, putting her in a chair.

He was gone for a few moments and she sat with closed eyes as the nightmare drained away, taking all the warmth from her body. But she opened her eyes when she felt him beside her again and looked up at him, in dull despair. 'Now,' he said, 'what's all this about?'

She should have said she was looking for something, the bathroom, and she slipped in the dark; but of course she couldn't lie about this and she said, 'I was sleepwalking.'

'Marvellous,' he said drily. 'Nobody mentioned this in your references.' Her head was clearing, aching but clearing, and there had been no deliberate deception. They probably hadn't known, if they had they would probably have forgotten.

She said, 'I was a child last time. It was over ten years ago. I couldn't have been much older than the twins.'

Her forehead was clammy when she touched it, like Peter's when she'd reached over the table to touch him on Saturday night.

'Well, I'm sorry,' said Gavin Tighe, 'but I wouldn't have much confidence in a sleepwalking nanny.'

'Of course not. I'll go in the morning. I don't know why——' She tried to think. She could remember it clearly and it had been in every detail like the old nightmares, except that she had never woken violently before. She had woken back in her own bed or being guided back by her mother who had treated the whole thing as a childish habit that Sophy would grow out of. She had thought she had outgrown it until tonight.

'Unhappiness, I suppose,' she said, to herself not to him. 'That was it before, I think, when I was a child.' Looking back, she knew that her sleepwalking phase had started when she had realised that she was the outsider. Cress was her father's favourite, Nick her mother's. She had learned to live with that and accept it. But the twins' unhappiness and her own rejection by Peter had merged together tonight.

She said, 'Being with Felicity and Charles today brought it back. They're unhappy children.' She was leaving in the morning and she wasn't afraid of him. 'They're afraid of you,' she added.

'Are they?' Perhaps he didn't know. More likely he didn't care.

'Didn't you know?' she asked, remembering the tear on Felicity's cheek. 'You were angry with them because we were out so long yesterday. Felicity cried when she told me.'

'She's quite an actress, is Felicity,' he said drily.

'If you say so.' She couldn't help them. She couldn't help anybody, not even herself.

'Miss Wade,' said Gavin Tighe, 'you have been conned.' She sat there, staring, and suddenly his voice sounded almost gentle. 'They think they're on to a soft touch with you.'

'But—they say you don't want them here!'

He grinned. 'The wicked uncle?'

'That they hate holidays. That they'd rather be at school?' That turned into a question as he went on smiling and she became less sure of her grounds.

'They love this house,' he said. 'Being here. What they don't want is supervision, because they prefer to be left to their own devilish devices. That was why they took you miles out of your way yesterday, to wear you out, to make you have second thoughts about the job.' Her mouth was falling open. 'You were lucky,' he told her. 'They led one poor woman so far astray we had to send out search parties.'

'I don't believe you.' But perhaps she did.

'It grieves me to say this,' he said, 'but my niece and nephew are two of nature's opportunists, and although God knows we need someone to help look after them I don't think you're quite up to it.' He was being nice. He was dismissing her, and she would have dismissed herself after tonight, but he was doing it gently.

She said, 'I hope it's true.' That the children were happy, and he knew what she meant,

'I'll prove it to you in the morning,' he said. 'Now you'd better get back to bed.'

She realised she had to be in his bedroom. The bed was behind them, sheets flung back when he must have leaped from it hearing her falling down the stairs. He was wearing a short robe and probably nothing else, and she got up quickly and muttered, 'Goodnight,' and was outside the door before she realised that she had no idea where she was.

She turned. 'I'm sorry, but I don't know which way to go.'

'Haven't you been round the house?'

'The twins showed me round yesterday, but they said they weren't allowed to open doors.'

He gave a hoot of laughter.

'Mrs Greenhaugh will be pleased to hear that! Come on.' He put a hand under her elbow, and Sophy felt it like a little electric shock.

'I hope I didn't wake the children,' she said.

'You didn't. I went to see.' As soon as he had put her in that chair, and that had to reassure her how he felt about them. She went with him, along corridors, up another short flight of stairs, and saw the light from the nursery door.

The children slept in the reflected glow, like rosy angels, and they had to be cherished and loved to look like this. She was so gullible, and now she had to leave in the morning. She had to go back home and admit having lost her job in one day because, as he'd said, what use was a sleepwalking nanny? She could have frightened the children to death.

She was useless, she was a hopeless case, and looking down at the sleeping Felicity, with no warning but a sudden catch of breath Sophy burst into a flood of tears. She thought Gavin Tighe had gone, but when she felt his hand on her shoulders she could only hiccup, 'Oh, God, I am such a mess!' and the tears wouldn't stop. She should have cried before for Peter instead of holding back. Now her heartache and the sleepwalking and her own stupidity crashed down on her together, and she ran from the children's bedroom and would have run across the nursery into her own room, but he was with her, and she was in another chair—the big armchair in the nursery now—and Gavin Tighe was saying, 'When you've finished crying we'll start talking.'

'There's nothing to talk about.' She didn't have a handkerchief, a tissue or anything. She was wearing only a cotton nightshirt and she put her arm across her face. She heard a door close, but although there was no other sound she knew that it was the door to the children's bedroom and he was still in this room with her. She could sense his nearness as she struggled for composure, and said at last, 'I'm not only a sleepwalker, I'm hysterical as well. Oh, boy, did you get a treasure!'

She had hit rock bottom. She couldn't make a bigger idiot of herself, and somehow that took away her selfconsciousness, and he said, 'That's better.'

'Better?' she echoed.

'You're smiling.'

'I'm not.' She wasn't smiling, but she might have been grimacing.

'Here,' he put a tissue in her hand, 'mop up.'

She could imagine him doing this for the twins. She blotted her face, blinked and dabbed her eyes, then blew her nose, and the crying jag was over. She looked for him and he was sitting down. 'We *have* had some treasures,' he said, in a conversational tone. 'There was one who was psychic and went round the house testing for cold spots. In the end she daren't come out of her bedroom. Mind you, the twins had told her there was murder done here.'

'Was there?' She didn't know whether to believe him or not.

'No,' he said. 'Grimm's fairytale stuff, only she hadn't read Bluebeard. Then there was Miss England, resting between engagements. She took two hours every morning putting on her face. She fascinated the twins, but she scared the daylights out of me.'

Sophy was giggling now, clutching her damp tissue, and when he smiled at her she ventured, 'I don't suppose I could stay and help in the house or the garden? I'm sure I won't be sleepwalking again, but I can see that I can't be in charge of the children. I wouldn't want paying even, just my meals and a bed, but it would mean an awful lot to me not to have to go home and say I was out after only a few hours.' She made a helpless little gesture, shrugging, and letting her hands fall on her lap, as she pictured herself facing the family. 'Not that they'd be surprised.'

'Wouldn't they?'

'They know I'm a dead loss.'

'And what do they base that on?' He was watching her steadily, and she said quickly,

'I don't have a record or anything like that. I didn't forge my references, I've led a blameless life. It's just that my brother and sister are good at everything, and I'm the flop of the family. They were so surprised when they heard I'd got this job. It was the first time I've ever surprised them in my life.'

'Really?' One dark eyebrow quirked. 'I should have thought you were a rather surprising young woman,' and that made her laugh again at the idea of her astonishing anybody, let alone a man like him.

'Well,' she said, 'I suppose there aren't all that many sleepwalking nannies.'

'You're the first one I've come across. Tell me about your family.'

'You're sure?'

'I wouldn't ask if I didn't want to hear.' He seemed to mean it. Sophy was a good listener, everybody said so, but no one had ever listened to her before. 'Well,' she began, 'my father is Gilbert Wade. He's head of economics at our local Poly and he writes books, and articles. I've been typing them for him, but my sister types better than I do anyway.'

'Gilbert Wade,' Gavin repeated, the name obviously meaning nothing to him. 'What kind of books?'

'Textbooks. They sell quite well.' She went on, describing her family with admiration and love, accepting her own role, which had been inbred in her. She told him this time about the dolls in her mother's shop, and how the twins had the same round and perfect faces.

'But rather tougher than your average porcelain,' he said, and that she was beginning to believe. 'Do you work in the shop?'

'Oh no. Cressida does. She did before she was married and she's a junior partner now with my mother. I'm the clumsy one. I knocked an early Wedgwood vase off its pedestal walking round the shop.'

'Not so many people have done that either,' he commented. 'You *are* surprising.'

'And the aftershave in the bathroom here—I'm sorry about that. Was it very exclusive?'

'Compared with an early Wedgwood, peanuts.'

He wasn't laughing at her. He wasn't scoring off anything silly she said. He was smiling now, but he had listened attentively, and most of the time he hadn't smiled at all. She asked, 'Do you have a family, apart from the twins?'

'My mother died when my sister was born, my father about ten years ago. There was just my sister.' She didn't think then how incredible it was that they should be talking like this.

'You've never been married?' she asked him.

'No. Have you?' He probably expected her to smile, saying no to that, because he already had the story of her blameless and uneventful life. So she did try to smile, saying, 'No,' but she couldn't quite make it, and he was reading her face. He knew she was suffering, he must guess that she had been jilted, and she turned her face away and said in a small voice, 'That's another reason why I don't want to go back still amounting to nothing.'

'Don't underrate yourself.' His voice was strong and deep, and it dragged her head round again, to look at him, and for a moment his dark eyes held hers. Then he got up and said, 'I'll see you in the morning.'

'Please,' she whispered, and as the door closed behind him she said, 'Thank you.' She went into the twins' room. Neither had moved, they were still in deep sleep. Then she turned out the main light and went into her own bedroom and switched on the bedside lamp, then stood looking at her reflection in the oval glass over the little dressing table. It was the same face, moony old Sophy, no brains, no beauty.

She threw her head back, and her shoulders, looking up. She seemed to have spent most of her life ducking her head. Well, there was a man here she would have to look up to, who was a head and shoulders taller than she was. Her throat gleamed white and smooth and the clean line of her jaw seemed to belie the childlike roundness of her face.

'Don't underrate yourself,' he'd said. Gavin Tighe had given her the first advice that had not belittled her. Tomorrow he might send her home, but the hope that he might not sent her to bed to sleep peacefully till morning.

CHAPTER FOUR

SOPHY woke feeling less hopeful. She lay remembering all that had happened last night: the sleepwalking, the floods of tears, the talking. Mostly the talking when Gavin Tighe had listened to her and encouraged her, but she wondered now if he was just calming her down in case she started off again and disturbed the children.

He was fond of them, there was no doubt about that. And they *had* fooled her, she was as sure as could be of that as well, so she hadn't shown much gumption, and this morning she had very little hope that he would let her stay on in any capacity. Although she would cheerfully have scrubbed floors to avoid arriving back home today.

The bathroom was near. She left the nursery door open and washed quickly. As she came out she heard the children's voices and hurried back along the landing, her bare feet making no sound. They didn't hear her until she stood in their doorway and then the chattering stopped, cut off dead, and they looked exaggeratedly solemn.

Sophy wondered how long they could have kept up the ill-treated role. She could see clearly now how they were 'conning' her so that she would hop to their every whim.

They were behaving well. They washed, cleaned teeth, and were getting into their clothes while she went downstairs to the kitchen to ask Mrs Greenhaugh, 'Where do the children have breakfast?'

'Down here,' said Mrs Greenhaugh.

'Oh,' said Sophy. 'Only I wondered if they had to

stay in the nursery.'

'No.' Mrs Greenhaugh was stirring porridge. Through the open door Tom was moving around in the living room that led from the kitchen, and Sophy knew that Mrs Greenhaugh thought she was hopeless. The housekeeper didn't offer another word, just went on as though Sophy had left the kitchen, and it was a little like home. Nobody took much notice of Sophy there either.

'Don't underrate yourself,' Gavin Tighe had said last night, and that worked for him because everybody rated him as the man in charge. It was harder if everybody thought you were nothing.

The twins were dressed by now, and shining-faced. Their dark eyes fixed Sophy as she went back into the room and she said, 'Mrs Greenhaugh says you don't have to stay up here, so shall we go down to breakfast?'

They led the way, saying nothing. Felicity did a skipping dance down the stairs and into a small dining or breakfast room where Gavin Tighe was sitting at a table laid for four. He was at the end of his meal, with an almost empty coffee cup and several opened envelopes at his elbow.

Sophy supposed she hadn't expected to find him here, because her breath caught in her throat when she saw him. 'Sleep all right?' he asked her.

'Yes, thank you.' He was wearing a business suit now, grey and beautifully tailored, sitting well on his broad shoulders; and considering what a state she had been in last night she could remember in surprising detail how he had looked then, in dark blue short dressing jacket, lean muscular legs, the dark hairs on his chest. She wondered how he remembered her, wild and weeping, and wished she had stopped to put on some make-up.

'Sit down,' he said. The twins already had, side by side, Sophy took the chair that was left, the one without the bowl of cornflakes set in front of it. Gavin looked at the twins, who poured milk on their cereal and started to eat, keeping their heads down.

'Miss Wade——' he began.

'Sophy,' Sophy murmured automatically.

'Sophy,' he amended, 'could be leaving us.'

Her heart sank, although she had expected it, and she was wryly amused to see the twins look dismayed.

'You don't want that?' said Gavin.

'She's a good swimmer,' said Charles. 'And a good climber.'

'What have you been climbing?'

'Trees.'

'Of course.' Sophy knew he was hiding a smile but the children didn't. 'And what else did you have planned?'

She began to reel off the list. 'We thought we might take a day trip to the sea, then there's the lakes and the zoo.'

'That should cheer them up,' said Gavin gravely. The children sat clutching their spoons, with identical guarded expressions. 'Sophy's sorry for you,' he said. 'So sorry that she was awake half the night worrying about you.' They looked at each other then, both chewing on an underlip, and Gavin continued, 'But she isn't sure she can stay in a house where the children get beaten regularly.'

Eyes widened and mouths opened. They both shook their heads. 'We never said that,' Charles protested. 'Did you?' He turned to Felicity, who went on shaking her head vigorously.

'Charles is usually the practical one,' Gavin explained. 'Felicity's flights of fancy go over the top at times. Do I beat you?' He leaned towards them and they both dissolved into giggles. 'Well, don't press your luck,' he said. 'And if Sophy is persuaded to stay, behave yourselves. Starting now.' He got up, picking up his mail. 'Can I have a word?'

Sophy followed him, across the hall into the study. He closed the door after her and said, 'This sleepwalking. Last night was the first time since you were a child?'

It wasn't easy to look straight into his face. Last night she had been beyond shyness. Now she was seeing clearly, and he was powerful and very disturbingly male, but she had to meet his eyes, and she did.

'Honestly,' she said. 'I was eight, and it isn't going to happen again.' She was suddenly sure of that as though childhood had finally left her.

'There's an alarm system, from the nursery downstairs,' he told her. 'Mrs Greenhaugh and Tom say they're willing to have it linked to their room at nights.'

So Mrs Greenhaugh had heard about the sleepwalking. No wonder she was beyond words this morning! 'They must think I'm a nut-case,' sighed Sophy, and Gavin said drily,

'No, they think I'm the nut-case.' For letting her stay. A girl with this kind of problem had to be unstable. 'This may be very temporary, you understand?'

'Until you find someone else,' she said. 'Of course.'

'Which may not be so easy.' He smiled and she felt a weight slipping from her shoulders, and now was the time to face Mrs Greenhaugh too, while she was buoyed up with Gavin Tighe's confidence. He was trusting her with the children. He believed that last night was an isolated not-to-be-repeated incident, and she said, 'Thank you,' and held her head high as she walked out of the room.

Mrs Greenhaugh was dishing up the porridge into a blue-rimmed bowl in the kitchen, and Sophy said, 'About last night.'

'Just a minute.' She took the porridge in to Tom. As she came back Sophy said, 'It's over ten years since the last time, and it isn't going to happen again.'

'No—well, we hope not, don't we?' Mrs Greenhaugh stood, arms folded, surveying Sophy. Then she sighed deeply. 'Well, I suppose we'll manage. I hear the children have been having you on.'

'I thought they weren't wanted here,' said Sophy. 'They seemed so scared of him,' and Mrs Greenhaugh's face broke into a reluctant grin at the unlikeliness of that.

'There's many a man as is,' she conceded, 'but nobody in this house.' Her lips went on twitching, 'They saw you, you know, before she went into the water. They've done that trick before. Last summer Charles went down and came up under the bridge, and the poor soul who was looking after them didn't know he'd come up and she was screaming and carrying on, half demented.'

Sophy could imagine it. 'They got into trouble that time,' Mrs Greenhaugh added grimly. And serve them right, thought Sophy.

'They must hate nannies,' she said.

'I'm not over-struck on them myself.' Mrs Greenhaugh sounded long-suffering. 'The ones who are getting on can't keep up with the children. The young ones are flighty and never stop making eyes at the master.' She took another assessing look at Sophy. 'At least you don't seem that sort.'

'Flighty?' Sophy had to laugh. 'Hardly—but thank you for letting me stay.'

'Beggars can't be choosers,' said Mrs Greenhaugh, which seemed to sum it up. 'Tom saw you climbing the tree with them yesterday. Perhaps that's what they need, another child to play with.'

Sophy's lips parted in protest, but last night she had been caught up in a child's nightmare, so she smiled again and declined a cooked breakfast, and took a plate of toast and cup of coffee with her.

The children were into toast and marmalade. Sophy sat down and drank some of her coffee while they munched thoughtfully and silently. Today's schedule had been to check on the buses out of Witherstone and plan future escape expeditions, but now she said, 'I'd like to take another look around the house this morning—you know, open a few doors.' They grinned sheepishly. 'And talking of doors that don't open,' she went on, 'how about the key to the toy cupboard? Would you happen to know how to lay your hands on that?'

They knew. Sophy carried the breakfast things back into the kitchen, staying to wash up although a dishwasher was part of the fixtures; and when she went up to the nursery the door of the toy cupboard was open, and the twins were prepared to show and share their toys.

That was fun. There was a lot of laughing and screaming done as Sophy made a hit with the glove puppets. They liked the crocodile best, with snapping jaws. Of course children loved scaring, so long as it was fantasy, and now she could see those sketches they had made yesterday afternoon in a different light. They had sketched children in peril, but come night they had slept safe and secure.

They put the toys away at last and the children took her round the house, and this time she learned the layout. When she walked down the shallow flight of steps where she had fallen outside Gavin's door Sophy's thoughts winged back for a moment to the dark hours. 'This is Uncle Gavin's bedroom,' Felicity announced, flinging open the door, and Sophy glanced briefly across. She felt she knew the room well.

'Another bedroom,' said Felicity, opening the room next door.

'That's pretty,' said Sophy.

The house was furnished with an ageless elegance, and when they came to the big drawing room downstairs Sophy thought that her mother and Cress could have a field day in here. Genuine, all of it. Sophy was well informed on antiques. Nobody ever asked her opinion, but with her mother and Cress constantly talking antiques, going to auctions, buying, selling, some of the knowledge was bound to rub off on her.

Mrs Greenhaugh was dusting at the far end of the room and Sophy held back the twins. 'No further,' she said.

'We *can* go in,' Charles explained patiently.

'Not while I'm in charge,' said Sophy, and laughed. 'Maybe when you're very tired and moving slowly.' She looked at a Constable painting, at the Sheraton chairs, and Mrs Greenhaugh, who was proud of it all and appreciated appreciation in others said, 'Of course, your mother's in antiques, isn't she?' Sophy had told her that. 'Go into the garden,' said Mrs Greenhaugh to the twins. 'Tom's out there, so you mind what you're up to.'

'If you fall in the lake again,' said Sophy, 'I'm not jumping in after you!' The children went and Sophy walked into the room, towards Mrs Greenhaugh.

It was one of the most attractive rooms she had ever seen. Generations of Gavin Tighe's family must have contributed to this, she felt, and she picked up a little pottery figure of a seated man, wearing a turban and a flowing rich blue robe. He had a dark drooping moustache and slightly askew eyes, and he made her smile, 'This is a nice bit of Staffordshire. Isn't he splendid? Oh, I *like* him!' There were pieces in here worth much more, but the Turk was charming. A one-time fairing, costing a few pence, now it would be worth anything up to eighty pounds. Sophy put him back and said, 'I suppose all this has always been here?'

'Two hundred years and more the house,' said Mrs Greenhaugh. 'There was a textile mill once, the lake was a mill stream. That went after the first world war. Then the engineering works opened. Old Charles was a clever man.'

'He was Mr Tighe's——?'

'Grandfather. It was his father who——' Mrs Greenhaugh sighed for what Gavin's father had done, or left undone. 'When Mr Gavin took over there wasn't much left in here nor much being done at the works. But he got this place back into shape,' said Mrs Greenhaugh with undisguised satisfaction. 'And there are two factories now. We've been here thirty years, Tom and me.' We're family, was her attitude, in tough times and good, and Sophy found that touching and thought she would like Mrs Greenhaugh to tell her more about the bad days, and how Gavin—who must have been about twenty when his father died—had set about restoring this house and an almost bankrupt business.

She walked around, remarking on anything that took her fancy. It was amusing to realise that compared with most folk she was an expert. She was impressing Mrs Greenhaugh by translating hallmarks, pointing out designers' stamps.

There were a few family portraits about. A pastel study of the woman who was Gavin's mother, with dark waving hair, and a pure youthful profile; and a laughing photograph of a girl with dark curls, 'Susanna,' said Mrs Greenhaugh. The twins' mother, Gavin's sister; the likeness to the children was striking.

'She was very pretty,' said Sophy.

'Life can be cruel,' said Mrs Greenhaugh.

'Yes.' Sophy thought of Peter and pain showed in her face, then the door opened and a girl came in with long strides that brought her right up to Sophy. 'Hello, Mrs G.,' she said cheerfully, and to Sophy, 'Hello, have you come to look after the brats?'

She was stunning. Her skin was tanned golden and her hair—even thicker and more luxurious than Cress's—was silver-gilt. She had high cheekbones and a hungry mouth and Sophy thought crazily 'It's Miss England, probably Miss World by now.' 'The twins,' she sounded as if she was stammering. She wasn't, but the words were sticking. 'Yes, that's right.'

The girl was eyeing her from head to foot, with a smile that grew wider all the time, and Sophy knew that this was because the girl thought Sophy looked a frump. 'Good,' said the girl, 'and good luck. I'm Judith, by the way—Judith Gretton. Gavin may have mentioned me.'

'I'm Sophy Wade,' mumbled Sophy, 'and no, he hasn't.'

'Why should he, come to think of it? I'm no part of the job.' She had rings on every finger, silver against her smooth brown hands. She wore no other jewellery, and she was very much at home here. When Sophy replaced the silver-framed photograph of Susanna Judith adjusted its position by a fraction as if Sophy had spoiled a pattern.

Suddenly a frown creased her smooth brow, and she stared even harder at Sophy, demanding, 'You're not expecting, are you?'

'Expecting what?' asked Sophy like an idiot, and Judith clapped a hand over her mouth.

'Whoops, sorry!' She was laughing now and Sophy was blushing furiously. 'I just called in to see what the latest was like,' said Judith. 'It's almost impossible to get good temporary staff, but I'm sure Sophy will fit in. 'Bye for now, then.'

Sophy put her hands on her hips, nipping in her billowing dress. Her waist was as narrow and her stomach was as flat as Judith's, and she was fuming. 'Cheek!' she glared at the closed door. 'Who's she?'

'Mr Gavin's young lady,' said Mrs Greenhaugh. 'That frock would look better with a belt.'

Sophy looked down at herself, 'I don't go in much for belts, but after that I see what you mean. Will the children be all right if I run upstairs and see what I can do?' She was suddenly anxious about her appearance. She had arrived here on Sunday, without even a touch of make-up on her face, and the dip in the lake had dulled and tousled her hair. God knows what she had looked like last night, and this morning she was still without make-up, but she resented Judith Thingummy's laughter at her expense.

She tied a scarf round her waist as a cummerbund, and put on make-up quickly. She had spent a lot of time on her face before her dates with Peter, although he had still decided he didn't want to see her face on his pillow. Gavin Tighe had told the reporter he didn't believe in marriage either, but probably neither did Judith, and Sophy was sure that had never stopped them sharing a pillow.

They would look wonderful together—Gavin as he was last night, but without the short dark robe, and Judith was probably that lovely golden colour all over. Sophy brushed her hair down, then tried to flip it up, finally ran her fingers through it, and because she was still warm with indignation she certainly looked livelier than usual. She thought, I wish I looked like she does, I wish he . . .

She put down the brush with a little bang and went off to find the children, before that second wish could form itself in her mind.

The children were batting a yellow ball to and fro across the lawn. When they saw Sophy they came to meet her, swinging small racquets. 'She's gone,' said Felicity. 'Did you see her?'

'Judith? Yes.'

'She's going to marry Uncle Gavin.' Felicity took a swipe at thin air as though she was swatting it. It was odd, but this seemed wrong, like a psychic warning of disaster. Sophy was not psychic, and she really knew very little about either of them, they could be ideally suited, but she did feel suddenly dejected. 'That *will* be nice,' she said.

'Well,' said Felicity, 'she's always here. And he takes her out a lot. And when there are people she's always here. And she stays for breakfast sometimes.'

'I'm sure a lot of people do,' said Sophy hastily.

'Not in the room next to Uncle Gavin's,' said Felicity.

'Well, it's none of our business,' said Sophy. 'Come on, I'll take the pair of you on at tennis.'

She could follow the flight of the bright yellow ball easily enough and the pace was almost pat-a-ball. Not all the time, the children had the makings of a couple of first class players, getting in the occasional smash, and more than once colliding with each other in their over-eagerness.

Sophy played a creditable game. Nobody was laughing at her here and when she wasn't selfconscious she was light and quick on her feet. She tried to lob fairly, first to one then the other, and her main handicap was her full skirt, which she tried hitching over her cummberbund until Charles asked reasonably, 'Don't you have some shorts or something?'

'Yes, I do. I'll change.'

The shorts were white and brief and she had only worn them once, six weeks ago, when Peter had attempted to teach her squash. Cress and Nick had warned him she was hopeless at any sport but swimming, but Peter had said it was worth a try, and Sophy's spectacles had slipped down her nose and she had shown no whit of promise in half an hour's tuition.

When she went out into the garden again the twins gave her a wolf whistle, and she said, 'Thank you very much. I wish I was a bit browner,' thinking of Judith's glowing skin.

They whacked the ball around until the twins began to flag, and Felicity flopped down, squinting up at Sophy and telling her, 'You look prettier today.' It was the make-up, of course, and the exercise. 'Yesterday you looked drippy,' Felicity announced, and Sophy jerked up howling in mock indignation.

'I should just think I did look drippy! I'd just dived into the lake after you and Mrs Greenhaugh told me you fell in on purpose, and you——' she jabbed an accusing finger at Charles, 'scared one poor girl silly because you came up under the bridge and she thought you were still down there. So watch it, the pair of you, because I have your measure!'

'That time,' said Charles, 'he really was mad at us.' They grimaced together and Sophy said severely,

'No more than you deserved,' and they both nodded, agreeing on that.

She went into the kitchen to bring out glasses of milk, and Mrs Greenhaugh chuckled at her ab-breviated shorts, 'Miss Gretton wouldn't be wondering

if you were expecting if she saw you in those! She
wouldn't be too pleased, though. Too good a figure.'
Sophy blushed again, peony-pink, and Mrs
Greenhaugh approved of that. She considered most
girls too hard-faced by half these days.

She was also pleased at Sophy's offer to turn her
hand to anything that needed doing. The way Sophy
had handled and discussed Mrs Greenhaugh's treasures had earned Mrs Greenhaugh's esteem. The little
Turk was one of her favourites, she had warmed to
Sophy's smile when the girl held him in her hand.
This was a sensible lass. 'You could help me wash
some of the china tomorrow if you liked,' she said, and
Sophy gulped, then said, 'I'd love to.'

Her family said she had two left hands as well as two
left feet, but Gavin Tighe had said, 'Don't underrate
yourself,' and when she looked her hands were steady.

After lunch Sophy took the children into the village
to check on the bus timetables. It was a poor service,
but she made a note of what there was, and the
children skipped along beside her and she was getting
more attention than she had ever had. Not for herself,
of course, but because she was with Gavin Tighe's
wards and must be the new nanny for the holidays.
She was young, so they were probably wondering if
she was another of the 'flighty ones', which sounded a
good old-fashioned word for someone who had a lot of
fun. Judith's approval had been no compliment. She
had considered Sophy so shapeless that she looked
pregnant, and Sophy went into the small wool and
haberdashery shop and asked if they sold belts.

The selection was limited, but she came out with a
wide white plastic one resolving to buy something
nicer as soon as she could. It was a small village, but
they wandered along the side lanes and the twins were
happy as sandboys. Sophy would have been happy

herself—on their good behaviour they were funny and sweet, and very bright—if it hadn't been for Peter.

She wouldn't sleepwalk again, she *must not*, but when she was alone tonight the black depression would return. It was waiting all the time, a little cloud that could cover the sky.

After the children had had supper she phoned home and got her father. 'It's Sophy,' she said. 'I just rang to say I've arrived and I'm settling in.'

'Ah,' said her father. 'That's right. That's good.'

'Everything all right at home?'

'Yes.' A moment's pause, then he repeated, 'Yes,' because he could never find much to say to Sophy. 'Your mother isn't home yet,' he added.

'I'll phone again,' said Sophy. She could imagine him replacing the receiver with relieved alacrity, although if she had been Cress he would have wanted to hear all about this family she was working for. He would have found something to talk about, if it was only the weather.

Felicity was sitting on the bottom of the stairs playing cat's cradle with a piece of string. Without looking up, still weaving the string around her small thin fingers, she said, 'That didn't take long.'

'They just wanted to know I was all right,' said Sophy.

She had hoped that Peter might ring today. Several times the phone had rung and someone had answered it, and Sophy had breathed a silent prayer. But it was never for her, and perhaps she was hoping too soon. Maybe towards the end of the week he would ring.

'Are you waiting for a phone call?' asked Felicity, and Sophy realised that she was hovering, looking down wistfully at the silent telephone.

'Not particularly,' she said. 'Why?'

'Because you go quiet every time it rings,' said

Felicity. They were shrewd youngsters. She must try not to be so transparent that a child of seven could see through her, but there was no point in denying it, so she said, 'It would be nice if it rang for me. Now come and have your baths, I've thought of a rather special bedtime story.'

When they were tucked up she sat on the end of Felicity's bed and started with a shipwreck. She made it very dramatic—lightning flashing, thunder crashing, mountainous waves, and two children, a boy and a girl, being washed up alone and defenceless on an island.

She described the island vividly. Tomorrow she would show them how to draw it, like the country of mythical monsters on her bedroom wall at home. There could be a fresh adventure every night. Tonight they met the fire-breathing dragon that roamed the coastline, and he turned out to be quite a friendly fellow.

The king of the island was the Tyger, who lived in the deep dark jungle, and whom she was saving. When she reached the end of tonight's episode she tucked them both in, and Felicity held up her face to be kissed. Charles didn't, but he snuggled down and mumbled, ''Night,' and Sophy felt that tonight, for now, they were both content to have her around.

As she walked back into the nursery she saw Gavin sitting in the armchair and stifled a yelp of surprise. He must have been listening to her. It didn't matter, she had been telling a childish tale for children, but she had been making rather a production of it. 'How long have you been there?' she asked.

'About ten minutes. You tell a good story.' He was smiling, and she smiled back.

'I'm not making it all up. I've got the map at home. I've had it for years on my bedroom wall. I used to imagine myself into it often when I was a child. I had all sorts of adventures.'

In her dreams Peter had always been with her, and she wanted to change the subject. She said, 'We went to look up the local bus timetable today. Would it be all right if we took some trips?'

'Of course.' He must be up here to say goodnight to the children. He would do that and then he would leave, but at the moment he was making no move to do either; and yet she could hardly sit down and make herself comfortable as if he was here to see her and they were about to spend some time together. 'You can use the car,' he said. 'You do drive?'

Here came a snag. 'Well,' she said, 'I do have my licence, but I am a little out of practice,' and then he stood up,

'Let's see, shall we?'

'You mean you want me to drive a car?' Sophy's voice rose.

'Yes.'

'Now?'

'No time like it.'

It would be like taking her test all over again. Worse, with Gavin Tighe sitting beside her, because she had passed that test, but she had serious doubts whether she would pass this. She croaked, 'Will the children be all right?'

'Mrs Greenhaugh will look in on them.'

He went into the children's room. They had heard what was going on. They were sitting up, waiting for him, and they threw themselves at him, Felicity's arms going around his neck, Charles hanging on to his arm. He hugged them both and Sophy felt a lump in her throat. Nobody had ever hugged her, and she envied them this kind of comfort.

'Sophy's going to try out the car,' he said, 'and then

perhaps she'll take you out tomorrow. No getting out of bed—Mrs G. is listening.'

Downstairs, after Mrs Greenhaugh had been alerted. Sophy started to explain, 'I've hardly done any driving since I passed my test. My brother let me borrow his car, but I scraped the paint against the gate, and I drove my mother around for a while, but I made her nervous.'

'I'm not a nervous man,' said Gavin, 'so let's see what you can do.'

She hadn't been in the garages. They were around the back of the house, and there were three cars: the black Mercedes, a red sports car and a Mini. 'Which one?' he asked, as though she might say, 'Oh, I'll take the Merc,' or, 'The red looks my kind of car.' She said, 'The Mini, of course, and please could you get me out of the garage?'

That wasn't making a good first impression, but she wasn't risking starting up in an enclosed space. Gavin couldn't use the Mini often. He had to bend nearly double to get into the driving seat, and she might have smiled if she hadn't been so tensed up. He drove the car out of the garage, got out of the driving seat and eased himself into the passenger's, and Sophy climbed in beside him, clutching her spectacle case. Her father had bought her contact lenses last Christmas, but she rarely wore them.

'I'm shortsighted,' she explained. 'I need these for driving and watching television.' She put on her glasses and blinked at him. They made his face even clearer, although she had always seen it clearly enough. If she never saw him again, after she left here, it would always be indelibly printed on her mind.

She was about to drive like a novice, which she was, of course, although she had passed her test first time, and her driving instructor had been quite pleased with her. If she could just pretend it was her instructor sitting beside her. He had been a whiskery old man who wore a hairy ginger suit and called her 'm' dear', and in every way he had been different from Gavin.

She couldn't even turn the ignition key. It seemed stuck, and the more she fumbled the more stubborn it proved. Perhaps it *was* stuck. She must have jammed it somehow. 'What's frightening you?' His voice was deep and slow, and she was frightened because she was a rotten driver and about to make a show of herself again. 'You do have a driving licence?'

'*Yes.*' Right there, in her wallet, if he wanted to see it.

'Have you ever had a bad accident?'

Sophy gave up trying to turn on the ignition and gripped the wheel instead. 'I've never had an accident at all, except for scraping Nick's wing.'

'Then for God's sake relax!' He took her hands from the wheel. They were trying to shake, but as he held them the shaking stopped as though some of his strength flowed into her. She thought, this is how the children must feel when he puts his arms around them and they know that everything is going to be all right. 'Easy does it,' he said, and this time the key turned when she touched it.

The car jerked forward, moving away, but after that she got round the house and down the drive, making the gear-changes smoothly, and drew up at the gates to ask, 'Which way?'

'Left.'

This was a nice little car, nearly new, the engine running beautifully. It was just the car she would have loved to own, only where would she have found the money to buy or maintain it? She asked, 'Who usually drives this?'

'Tom or Mrs G.'

'Are they good drivers?'

'Tom is. Mrs G. doesn't like driving.'

'I thought I didn't,' Sophy heard herself say. 'Although I quite enjoyed the lessons and it was lovely passing my test first time, but driving my mother I had one or two near misses.' She smiled at the memory of them, although she bit her lip. 'Nothing serious.' She remembered the sharp note in her mother's voice, 'Sophy, look *out!*' and then she would crash the gears or stall. But with Gavin sitting beside her, as relaxed as a six-foot-four man could be in the space allowed, she was driving smoothly, looking ahead; and when a Jag hooted behind her and came roaring alongside, with a blind bend clearly marked, she slowed down, holding back.

It was as well she did, because he skidded on the bend, narrowly missing the opposite ditch, brakes and tyres screaming. Then he revved up like mad, and zoomed away, making a V-gesture at Sophy, who had to do some quick manoeuvring to avoid him.

'Charming,' she said. 'Don't you meet them?'

'All the time,' said Gavin. 'Your mother must be very neurotic. You're an excellent driver.'

It was one of the nicest things anyone had ever said to her. She glowed with pleasure and started chattering, 'I'm enjoying this. Perhaps I'm not such a bad driver, I just need practice. Perhaps I need more practice in everything.'

'At nineteen,' he said, 'you've plenty of time.'

'I suppose so.' Life stretched ahead of her, like the road winding into the dusk of evening. But it would make all the difference who you travelled with, because Sophy didn't think she would enjoy travelling alone.

For half an hour she followed the route Gavin directed, her confidence boosted by the little episode with the young man in the Jag. That had got her adrenalin flowing and sharpened her reactions. Or perhaps it was all because Gavin Tighe was sitting beside her.

'We're here,' he said at last, and she saw that they were approaching the buildings that were the main branch of Tighe Industries. There were some lights on, but the gates were locked and a man came forward from a building beside the gates to identify them. Then the gates opened, and Sophy drove through, and asked, 'What are we here for?'

'I want to collect some papers.'

Night made it even more impressive. She could imagine how teeming and busy it would be in the daytime, but now everywhere echoed. The office block loomed ahead, and a security guard appeared as Gavin opened a side door. Sophy wondered if she should have stayed in the car. She had got out automatically when Gavin did, because she was curious, she wanted to see, and it would have been a little spooky, sitting out here in the Mini, in the middle of the vast silent complex.

She walked with Gavin, looking about her, although there wasn't much to see but closed doors, each with its own inscription. Then they reached the main entrance, and the security man who had come with them—Sophy caught him looking at her, wondering who she was—opened lift doors and ushered them in.

Up they went. She hadn't said anything. Gavin had said, 'All right, Jim?' to the security man, who had responded with, 'Right as rain, sir,' and as they walked from the side door to the lifts they had talked about his greyhound. Not Gavin's—Jim's. It appeared he had a greyhound, called Liddington Lurcher, that the lads had backed last Wednesday and that had come in second. It was doing all right and Jim was proud of it, and he beamed at Gavin's praise. Just like I did, thought Sophy. Gavin knows how to get the best out of people as well as machines.

As the lift rose higher, passing floor after floor, she asked, 'Is all this yours?'

'Most of it.'

She smiled wryly. 'My country's that map on my bedroom wall, all in my head. But yours is bricks and mortar and drawing offices and engineering works. Yours is real.' It was strange that she should be talking to him like this. Until lately she had done most of her talking in her head too. Now, with this man who ought to have frightened her silly, she was speaking her thoughts aloud.

'When I was your age,' he said, 'most of my world was in my head too.'

'It isn't now, though, is it? I wish you'd teach me some of the things you've learned.' The double edge of what she was saying struck her as she spoke. Not just the cheek of suggesting that a tycoon should waste his time showing her the way around but that she could have sounded sexually provocative.

'It would be my pleasure,' he said gravely, and smiled, and Sophy smiled back as though laughing when he laughed was natural because they were on the same wavelength. Her embarrassment dissolved and she was still smiling when the lift stopped and the door opened and Gavin waited for her to step out ahead.

His office windows must overlook the whole complex, but now it was dark out there. It was an impressive room, spacious and modern and functional. Quite different from the house with its antique treasures. He went across to a huge black and chrome desk, took some papers out of a drawer and began to go through them.

Sophy peered round an open door into what must be the boardroom. There was a long table that glimmered in the light from this room, with leather-backed chairs around it, and a bigger chair at the head. She could imagine Gavin sitting there, running the works, listening to advice and opinions from the men in the other chairs, but all the time knowing exactly what he was doing.

'My grandfather,' he said.

He was behind her, moving quietly over the carpeted floor, startling her so that she gasped, 'What?'

'Up there.' He pointed to an oil painting at the far end of the room. All she could make out was the pale blur of a face, and she hadn't been looking at the picture anyway, just at the empty chairman's chair. Now she went towards the painting and lights came on.

Gavin didn't follow her, so that when she turned they were on opposite ends of the long table. 'He wasn't very much like you,' she commented. The painting had shown a man with medium colouring and a pleasantly bland face. Although the eyes and the mouth looked shrewd there was no sign of the dark dynamism that characterised Gavin.

He said, 'He had some good ideas, but he was easily satisfied.' So this was old Joseph. Sophy said, 'You're not easily satisfied or there wouldn't be all this to show, would there?'

'I'm never satisfied,' and she could feel the restlessness, although he stood quite still. She spoke lightly, but she did wonder, 'Where do you go from here?'

'Right ahead,' he said, and she said,

'I wish you well.'

'Thank you.' Gavin turned in the doorway and she

hurried down the length of the long table, and when they were outside again she asked, 'Do I drive again?'

'Why not?'

She had confidence this time. She drove carefully and well, following directions again until they approached a pub, brightly lit, with cars in the parking lot, and he said, 'Pull in here. I could use a drink, could you?'

'A very small one.' She would like to sit and talk. She would like to walk into a crowded room with him. She parked neatly in the space vacated by a car that drew out as they drew in, and sat waiting while Gavin made his way to the bar.

A young man, sitting near, looked casually over her way and let out a howl, 'If it isn't Blondie! Bloody woman driver nearly had me off the road!' It was the road-hog in the Jag, with a flushed face that looked well over the alcohol limit but still seeing clearly enough to recognise Sophy.

'You could do with some driving lessons!' he roared, and suddenly Gavin was there, eyes glittering and mouth like a trap, leaning over the drunk, speaking softly and looking as menacing as a Mafia hit man.

'Any lessons being given round here, mate, will be the one I give you, if you'd like to come outside.'

Sophy could see the drunk taking in the height and the width of shoulders, and the face of the man who loomed over him. He cowered down into his chair, and Gavin said, 'Go easy on that,' meaning the glass on the table. 'You were a menace behind the wheel an hour ago. Kill yourself if you want to, it's the poor sods who might meet you I'm thinking of.'

The group around the drunk was getting the message. Everybody seemed to agree, and Gavin said to Sophy, 'There's a restaurant here, shall we eat?' She was glad to get up and follow him, and catching up she asked,

'Do they know you?'

'I shouldn't think so,' he said, 'I didn't know any of them.'

She knew that he hadn't been recognised, none of these men worked for him, but he had been recognised as too dangerous to tangle with. A waitress took them to a table, gave them menus, and walked away reluctantly while they selected, keeping her eyes on Gavin.

'Suppose he had gone outside,' Sophy pursued it, 'what would you have done?'

'Knocked him down,' said Gavin, and she gave a spurt of laughter.

'Sorry,' she said, although he was grinning too, 'but I'm trying to imagine my family's faces if they knew you'd invited somebody to step outside because he'd insulted my driving.'

There would be blank disbelief. They would consider the situation impossible. And that she should be sitting here now with the man who had been guest of honour on Saturday night; and who had done more for her confidence in twenty-four hours than anyone else in the whole of her nineteen years. Five weeks of being near Gavin, she thought, and it will be a very different woman who goes home and meets Peter again.

CHAPTER FIVE

ALL the time, during that meal, laughter was bubbling inside Sophy. If my friends could see me now! she kept thinking, and the most incredible thing was that she knew she wasn't boring Gavin. She was talking so easily, and he was talking to her as though she was the person he really wanted to be with. He could probably give that impression with anyone, it could be part of his success story, but it made her feel special.

She only had one glass of wine. It was the situation that was heady, that made the trout with shrimp sauce taste out of this world and the Black Forest Gateau melt on her tongue. On the way back the radio played and she got the car into the garage with no trouble at all.

Mrs Greenhaugh heard the front door opening and came down the hall as they went in. 'Never stirred,' she reported, looking towards the stairs. 'Tom went up five minutes ago.'

'Thank you,' said Gavin. He opened the study door and Sophy said, 'If you want any typing done, I can type.'

He had a staff of goodness knows how many who could type, but she meant here and now, anything connected with these papers, and he said, 'These are for reading, but some time I could take up your offer. Come here.' She followed him into the study, and Mrs Greenhaugh moved forward to stand in the doorway, and Gavin lifted a typewriter out of a cupboard and put it on a side desk.

It was an electric and Sophy used a manual, but

when Gavin said, 'You might try your hand with this tomorrow and get the feel of it,' she said, 'Sure,' quite breezily. She would get in some practice somehow. Once you'd adjusted your touch it had to be easier.

'Goodnight,' he said, and smiled at her, and outside in the hall Mrs Greenhaugh asked, 'Get on all right with the car?'

'Yes, thank you, it's a nice car. Then we went to the works, then we stopped at a pub and had something to eat.'

'Mmm,' said Mrs Greenhaugh, and Sophy thought, she's wondering if I'm going to be another of the young ones who 'make eyes at the master'. 'Give you a bit of advice,' said Mrs Greenhaugh, and Sophy knew what was coming, but she was wrong, because Mrs Greenhaugh chuckled, 'Keep out of Miss Gretton's way. You don't look like you did this morning. She might not be so pleased to see you next time!'

She went off down the hall, still chuckling, and Sophy went upstairs to the nursery and the children. They were sleeping, and she got ready to get into her own bed. The black despair didn't come down on her tonight, just a melancholy, as though Gavin Tighe had given her something to ease the pain. Some of his own life force, reminding her that she still had a life of her own. But she must never start reading anything in his dealings with her but kindness, because that would be the most stupid thing she could possibly do.

It was a good house to work in. Sophy found a niche in a dozen different ways. The children were her main task, of course, and she had a rapport going with them from the first day. They needed watching, she had to keep a jump ahead, but even before she took them swimming they had decided that in Sophy they had a good companion.

The weather was fine most of the time. It was turning into the loveliest spring she could remember, but it was not warm enough for swimming in the lake, although the twins assured her they did all the time in the summer holidays.

On Friday, the fifth morning of her stay, Sophy loaded them into the back of the Mini and drove to the nearest public baths, and they dived in like water babies. The only other swimmer was a youngish man who couldn't keep his eyes off Sophy. She had always known she was a good swimmer, of course, but she had been too inhibited to recognise the sexual response her nearly naked body evoked, and certainly too shy to deal with it. Now, in her new-found confidence, she was more than a match for the man who splashed up to ask, 'Yours, are they?'

'Oh yes,' she assured him, and he peered at her left hand.

'I don't see any ring.'

'No, but you should see their father,' she said, and swam away in a fast and perfect crawl.

Gavin was right, the twins were practically amphibious, but anything they could do Sophy could do better, and when she eventually dragged them out protesting Charles asked, 'Are you a champion?'

'Not me!'

'I bet you could be.'

'I'll bet you could.'

'Oh, we are. We're the school champions.'

So was I, she remembered, but it didn't count because my parents never managed to get along to the swimming sports. She asked, 'Does your uncle come to watch you?' and Felicity said, 'Of course.'

When Gavin came into the nursery that night, to say goodnight to the children, Charles informed him, 'Sophy took us swimming.'

'So I've been hearing,' said Gavin. She had the children out of the bath now, into pyjamas but still running around.

'A man asked her if we were hers,' Felicity piped up, 'and she said we were and he said he didn't see a ring, and she said no, but he should see our father.'

They had been underwater. She was sure they had, diving for a two-pence piece. But that must have been one of the moments Felicity popped up for air. 'Why should he see our father?' Felicity asked as though this had suddenly occurred to her as strange, and Charles said impatiently,

'*Silly*, she was putting him off. He fancied her. Of course she didn't fancy him, he could only do the breast-stroke, but he kept trying to touch her.'

Sophy coloured and gabbled, 'They are *fantastic* swimmers, *and* school champions, they tell me. I don't know who taught them, but——'

'He taught us,' said Felicity. Gavin said,

'With a lake in the garden there wasn't much choice,' and Sophy had a mental picture of him, gleaming wet from head to foot, in brief trunks, and of herself with regret because he would never see her the way that had made the man in the pool want to touch her.

'Sophy can somersault from the top board,' Charles announced, and Gavin said,

'I always knew she was a surprising lady. Would you do some typing for me tonight, Sophy?'

'I'd love to,' said Sophy.

There was the bedtime story to get over first. By now the map of the island was Blu-tacked to the nursery wall, and as the story advanced another 'monster' was drawn in. Tonight's was a great snake that Felicity had crayoned in green and scarlet, and Sophy sat on the edge of Felicity's bed and took the children with her on tonight's adventure.

Gavin hadn't sat in on another session since that first night, and she was glad he hadn't. It was fun to hold two children in shivering thrall and send them happy to sleep, but once was enough with a sophisticated adult.

Before she went downstairs Sophy went into her own bedroom and touched up her make-up. She had taken such care with her appearance during the two months that Peter was dating her, but somehow the effect had been different. The cosmetics were the same, except that she was using eye-shadow now with more flair, but now she held herself differently, her head higher and her shoulders pulled back. She was surprising herself constantly, as Gavin pretended she was surprising him, and this was the first time he had asked her to do any typing, and she was ready.

She had practised a little each day, and this machine went like a dream so that her speed doubled and trebled. After the first day she stopped copy-typing and began to type out whatever came into her head: words of songs, lines of poetry, letters to friends which she posted later. She didn't write to Peter, and she didn't write home because she would be phoning home on Sunday and there was nothing she could say to Peter. The next move had to come from him.

She hadn't told anyone that she was working for Gavin Tighe, but yesterday she had typed his name and sat back and looked at it on the clean white sheet of paper, at a loss what to type next. She had pulled that sheet of paper out of the typewriter and dropped it into the wastepaper basket that she took down to the kitchen and emptied at the end of each session.

Now she looked at her reflection in the mirror and saw a wide and happy grin. She was about to show Gavin something else she could do well, type, and although that was no earthshaking talent it would make her feel good. She had been starved of praise all her life. She was blooming under a touch of appreciation, because even when he was dating her almost every day Peter had still thought she was thick. So did I, thought Sophy, but Gavin doesn't, and why shouldn't Gavin be right about me when he's right about almost everything?

She tapped on the study door and he looked up from the desk, and her heart gave the little skip of pleasure that she often got just looking at him. There were papers by her typewriter, and he said, 'If you'd make a copy of those for me.'

'Of course.'

It was a report on a proposed building extension, with notes written in the margin by most paragraphs. Sophy had to incorporate the notes and she started slowly, having him in the room made her careful, but soon she was tapping briskly away, and when she finished a page Gavin said, 'Let me see. Very good,' he said when she put it in front of him, and when she blinked suddenly, 'Something in your eye?'

'My contact lenses, I'm trying to master them. I need to see my way around here and spectacles slip down my nose after a while.'

There were treasures about. She was allowed to dust and handle all sorts of exquisite pieces. She had never mentioned the shattered Wedgwood to Mrs Greenhaugh, but because of it she was learning to live with her lenses.

'With the twins around I know what you mean,' said Gavin, and of course there was that too. She needed good eyesight here.

It took her almost an hour to finish, while he sat at his desk working his way through another pile of papers. When she said, 'That's it,' he said, 'That's it for me too,' and got up and came over, checking her typing, quickly but she knew he would have spotted any error.

When she stood up she supported her back with her hands, arching backwards. She had stiffened, hunched over the typewriter, concentrating on making that copy a hundred per cent accurate. 'I think my backbone's locked,' she murmured, and Gavin said, 'I have a cure for that.'

'W—what?'

'A walk round the garden.'

'Oh, yes. Yes, that would be nice.' It was a mild evening, a stroll in the moonlight would be lovely, but for a mad moment she had thought he might be going to take her in his arms and run his fingers down her spine. Her nerve ends tingled as though he had, and she felt frissons of sensation running up and down her vertebrae. She loved Peter. It had always been Peter. But now she was being thrown into close and daily contact with a man whose sensual magnetism was on a par with the power he wielded, and of course she was stirred by him. This was her first experience of lust, although she recognised it for what it was and it might be perilous, but it was thrilling. It made her feel dangerously alive.

They walked into the cool gardens, talking about the twins and whether Sophy could drive them into Buxham tomorrow. She had her first week's pay and she wanted to do some shopping. The clothes she had brought with her seemed so dull, and she had a hankering for something bright and pretty. Suddenly she didn't care if she did stand out in the crowd.

Gavin's permission to take the children was automatic. He simply said, 'Of course,' and Sophy said, 'I'm sorry Felicity heard what I said to that man about her father. I didn't know she had. Like Charles said, I was just hoping it would make him keep his distance.'

'It didn't seem to work.' He was smiling at her, and she grinned.

'Again, like Charles said, he wasn't much of a swimmer. Most of the time I could outdistance him.' When she had said, 'You should see their father,' she was thinking of Gavin, their surrogate father, who had scared off the last man who pestered her. 'Is it likely to upset them?' she asked.

'No,' he said. They were walking over the bridge over the lake now. Water shimmered beneath them and above the sky sparkled with stars. 'They were only months old when their parents died, this has always been their home.'

Sophy looked at the stars in the lake and thought of bright lights extinguished, that laughing girl in the photograph, and said quietly, 'She was very beautiful.'

'Yes,' he said. 'They should have had their lives in front of them. It was a wicked waste.' She would have liked to put a hand on his arm, to comfort him, and he looked down at her and it was as though he knew that although they didn't touch.

They walked on almost silently and for Sophy there was a wonderful feeling of companionship. In the car, when he took her home that first day, there had been no communication, but then she had known that he had cut her out of his mind. Now they were together. He was aware of her, and she was so aware of him that it was as though she breathed him in with the cool night air and he filled her with well-being.

They crossed the bridge and strolled under the trees, just walking close, brushing occasionally, exchanging a word and listening to the sounds of silence. Then back to the house.

A phone began to ring as they went in. Gavin answered it in the hall and Sophy waited, as she always did for a moment because it might have been

Peter. Peter was her real love. Gavin was so far out of reach that all she could ever feel for him was infatuation, and she must keep that in check.

But the call was not for Sophy, and from the sound of Gavin's voice it was Judith. Sophy ran up the stairs back to the nursery, so fast that her heart was thudding when she reached her own bedroom. They had walked like friends just now, but she wished he had held her arm, and turned her towards him and kissed her out there in the garden.

Perhaps he hadn't wanted to. She would have taken that for granted a week ago, but since she had been in this house a sensual awakening was taking place in her, and although she knew that Gavin would never risk getting really involved with her she also knew that he found her attractive.

She wondered, not for the first time, how it must be to be Judith, and was shaken with yearning so that she frightened herself and shot into the bathroom and washed her hair and concentrated on getting it into shape. She had tied it back with a scarf, after showering, after swimming, and that was another thing. Since she felt she was looking quite fetching she had even found it easier to manage her hair.

I don't know about getting a wage, she thought, sitting at her dressing table, brushing her hair. I think I ought to be paying somebody for what's happening to me here!

She hadn't met Judith again, although Judith had been downstairs only yesterday talking to Mrs Greenhaugh and waiting for Gavin to come home. Sophy hadn't dodged her exactly, just kept out of her way, because if anyone here could blight her growing confidence that person would be Judith Gretton.

On Sunday she phoned home and spoke to her mother and told her that things were going well. Since

Sophy had gone away Sara Wade had begun to realise how useful she had been, so she would have been quite relieved to hear that snags had developed in this job and Sophy was on her way home, but she was not admitting that. She passed on the family news— everyone was well, Cress was having her lounge redecorated—then she asked 'Heard anything from Peter?'

'No,' Sophy had to admit. 'He hasn't been in touch at all.'

She had bought a red dress in Buxham. She never wore red, Peter liked her best in blue, but she had wanted this dress as soon as she saw it yesterday, and everyone here said it suited her. She was wearing it now.

'Will you be coming home next weekend?' her mother asked.

'I don't think so.'

'The weekend after? That's Easter. You might be able to do an hour or two in the garden. Nick and your father are very busy, the lawns are starting to grow and you know it's impossible to get a gardener.'

Sophy felt a pang for her garden, and a flare of irritation towards Nick who had as much spare time as the next young professional man, and could have mowed the lawn instead of playing squash or entertaining his girl-friends one evening. When she saw him she would tell him that, but she didn't want to commit herself to a date for going home, so she said, 'We're doing something special for Easter.'

Her mother didn't bother to ask what. She said, 'Well, take care of yourself, dear,' and Sophy sighed as she put down the phone and Felicity enquired,

'What *are* we doing for Easter?'

'You'll see,' promised Sophy, not having a clue.

'Who hasn't been in touch at all?' asked Felicity.

'A friend. Why are you always sitting on the stairs when I make a phone call?'

'I'm not!' protested Felicity in injured tones. 'Not always I'm not.'

As Sophy had only made two calls perhaps she was being unduly carping, so she laughed, 'You're just born nosey, are you?' and Felicity giggled.

'We're doing something special for Easter,' Charles told Gavin that evening when he looked in the nursery to say goodnight, and Gavin turned to Sophy, who stammered, 'It's—er—a surprise.'

A few minutes later, with the children in bed and the door closed on them, Gavin asked, 'What's this Easter surprise?' and she had to admit, 'I don't know. It was a sort of rash promise. Do you have anything arranged for Easter?'

'No,' he said, 'so you'd better start thinking.'

They lacked for nothing, these children, but they weren't spoiled, they could turn most things into an adventure. 'I suppose,' said Sophy, 'I could take them to the egg rolling.' She began to gather up the day's washing: socks, jeans, vests, sweaters, and explained, 'They have that each Easter Sunday where I come from. It's held in the park. The children decorate hardboiled eggs and roll them down this steep hill, and when the eggs get smashed you eat them. It's a laugh, I've been along with friends and their children. Do you think that would be all right? It's a very old custom. It goes back to the Middle Ages.'

'Educational as well,' commented Gavin. 'By all means take them to the egg rolling.'

Even when he was smiling he still looked tougher than any other man she knew, but she really did like his smile, and at the time the Easter egg rolling seemed a good idea. But afterwards she wished she

had come up with something else, because if she
arrived in her home town she was bound to meet
someone she knew, and she would have to call in at
home. She didn't want to go back home yet, although
by Easter weekend she would have been away for three
weeks.

They were almost completely carefree weeks.
Sophy's grief at losing Peter was always at the back of
her mind, but she had hopes, and this was more like a
holiday than a job of work. She spent hours on the
moors, until she knew them almost as well as the
children did. She helped Mrs Greenhaugh in the house
and Tom Greenhaugh in the garden, and being with
Gavin, copy-typing for him, even thinking about him,
put a sparkle into her life. It could do no harm,
admiring him, fancying him, because it was only for a
few more weeks, and then she would go home and this
would be like a schoolgirl crush, a happy memory to
look back on.

Not that it was all easy going with Gavin. Some
days he came back to the house in a black mood and
shut himself in his study or set off to walk alone over
the moors. Mrs Greenhaugh warned Sophy, 'He's got
things on his mind,' and over the breakfast table he
was amiable again and obviously more than capable to
dealing with the hitch or the problem that had plagued
him last night.

Some days he didn't come back. Sophy could hardly
enquire if it was work or Judith that kept him all
night, but she missed him nearly as much as the
children did. Not in the way she missed Peter, of
course, but when Gavin was in the house it was like an
extra charge of electricity in the air.

Charles was practical about the egg rolling. 'Do we
have to eat them all?' he wanted to know. 'I don't
think I can manage more than two.'

'We'll bring the rest back,' said Sophy, 'and put them in a salad.'

They spent most of Easter Saturday preparing the eggs, boiling them in vegetable dyes, painting faces and patterns with fibre-tipped pens. Mrs Greenhaugh recalled that boiling with onion skins gave eggshells a pretty marbled effect, and Gavin walked into the kitchen in the middle of the action.

Felicity was working with fierce concentration, painting red eyes on a bright green egg, while Charles was doing a checkerboard design. 'What's all this?' enquired Gavin. 'A new cottage industry?'

'Eggs for the egg rolling,' Sophy reminded him.

'Mine's the Hulk,' said Felicity.

'Very artistic.' Gavin sat down and made a clown face. Sophy was painting a heart on her egg. 'Nobody's going to smash you up,' Felicity promised Hulk, and Sophy looked at her heart and thought, I wish I could feel as sure.

She might see Peter tomorrow, and he might find her changed and more attractive, but she wasn't all that hopeful after what Cress had told her this morning, when she rang the shop to tell her mother she would be bringing the twins along for lunch tomorrow.

Cress had answered the phone, and Cress had said, 'Peter's going around with Anne Marie again.' She had said other things too, like she might get over to see Sophy for a few minutes, and the decorators were doing her bedrooms now, having finished downstairs, and everybody was well.

Anne Marie had been one of Peter's earlier girl-friends and there was no reason why he shouldn't be dating her again, and that would be a reason why he hadn't phoned Sophy. But it still gave Sophy a little stab of pain. So did Cress's voice, although she had heard that tone of malicious glee often enough before. Perhaps Sophy was hearing clearer, seeing things as they were, but that was when she realised that her lovely sister *was* malicious, a stirrer, pampered and not very kind.

She looked down now at the heart she was painting and sighed, and Gavin asked, 'Are you sure it's hardboiled?'

'It had better be!' Sophy managed a grin. 'There's no future for the soft-centred in this game!'

Next morning she put on a scarlet turtle-necked sweater, but not one of the bulky kind that she used to wear. This was ribbed and slick and worn with a wide patent scarlet belt, a straight grey flannel skirt and a pair of soft grey leather boots. The skirt had a side split so that she could stride around, and she slung a scarlet shoulder bag over her shoulder, picked up the basket of painted eggs and said goodbye for now to Mrs Greenhaugh and Tom.

'Have a good time,' said Mrs Greenhaugh, 'and don't get eating too many of those things and giving yourself the stomach-ache.' She sneezed, and both twins blessed her, and Sophy asked anxiously, 'Are you getting a cold?'

Mrs Greenhaugh thought it was nice that Sophy was concerned and said affably, 'Mr Gavin said give him a knock when you're ready to go. He's in the study.' Sophy presumed he wanted to say goodbye to them, he had finished breakfast when they came down, and she tapped on his door and the twins piled into the room.

He was at the desk, the inevitable paperwork before him, but he got up as they went in. 'We're going now,' said Sophy.

'Come on, then.' He led the way out to the garages. She had been going to take the Mini, but he opened the Mercedes and ushered the children into the back seat, and Sophy stammered, 'You're not letting me drive this? Honestly, I'd rather not.'

'So would I,' he said. 'I'll be doing the driving. One of the few things I haven't seen is an egg rolling.'

The twins squealed approval and Sophy felt joy whoosh through her. 'Oh *yes!*' she said. 'Oh, you *should* come with us.' She slipped into the passenger seat and hugged herself because she had very nearly flipped and hugged him. Her turning up with Gavin Tighe was going to blow her family's mind. This would show them all. She would never be moony old Sophy again.

But none of that mattered. If they had been on their way to picnic on a lonely beach she would have been just as delighted to have him along. She was so euphoric at the prospect of hours with Gavin, and nothing to do but talk and watch the children and be happy, that it was a good five minutes before she began to think of anything else.

The fine weather had brought out the crowds. Wet Easters could make the egg rolling a miserable affair, with bored parents and disappointed children. But today was, so far as Sophy could see, absolutely perfect. They left the car and strolled across the park, exchanging smiles with parents, and she felt, just for today, that this was her family—this beautiful boy and girl, and this handsome man. She felt tall and beautiful herself, and as they climbed the hill— dodging the down-coming eggs and the children running beside them—she thought she would never forget a single detail. That every colour and every sound would stay in her mind for ever.

Those who strolled into the park as onlookers sat and stood around, watching and chatting. Most of the parents stayed at the top of the hill with the baskets, scrambling down to pick up children who tripped or to retrieve smashed eggs.

A freckled wiry little boy boasted to Felicity, 'This is a sixer,' and Sophy explained, 'It's got to the bottom six times without getting smashed,' and Felicity tossed back her dark curls and her rosebud lips curved disdainfully. What a heartbreaker she's going to make, thought Sophy, proud as a mother, as Felicity carefully selected an egg from the basket as the little boy with his 'sixer' watched.

Charles got his first egg away with a gentle roll. Gavin, wearing a thin brown polo-necked sweater, a fine tweed jacket and brown slacks, was easily the most striking man there, and Sophy looked at both of them with delight, then someone touched her shoulder and said, 'It is Sophy, isn't it?'

Catherine Reid was a friend of Cress's. A double divorcee, still in her twenties, here with her current fiancé and his small sulky-looking daughter, Catherine looked the way she always did, expensive in exclusive casuals, her dark straight hair and her Bermuda tan completing the picture.

Catherine was cool, nothing ruffled Catherine, but now she was goggling at Sophy; and when she smiled at Gavin her eyes shone and her teeth gleamed. The fiancé was at the bottom of the hill, peeling eggs. Up here Catherine was fluttering her lashes at Gavin and saying archly, 'You must be Mr Greenhaugh.'

'Must I?' said Gavin.

When she knew Gavin was coming along Sophy had known she must explain. But it wasn't easy with the twins in the back of the car and she had had no chance since, so she explained to Catherine, 'Mrs Greenhaugh is the housekeeper. Mr Tighe is my employer.'

'Tighe?' Catherine's brow wrinkled. 'That sounds familiar.'

'Tighe Industries,' said Sophy.

'You're Gavin Tighe? Well, hello!' Catherine sounded as though she was greeting someone she had always wanted to meet, although if Gavin had been short and fat and balding she probably wouldn't have been batting her eyelashes like that.

Silly woman, thought Sophy, I always thought you were a silly cow. And it was true, although up till three weeks ago Catherine Reid could have had her blushing and stammering. This morning she only made Sophy smile, and at that moment a piercing scream rent the air.

Near the bottom of the hill Felicity, who was doing the screaming, was taking a swing at the boy with the 'sixer', and Gavin said, 'Excuse me.' Catherine's honeyed tones became brisker as she watched him go down the hill.

'Well, you've certainly changed!' she drawled.

'Yes, I have.' Sophy couldn't have agreed more.

'Cress told us you were working for——'

'Mrs Greenhaugh,' said Sophy. 'In a way I am. He just happens to be her boss too.'

'Are they his children?' Catherine was getting in all the questions she could before her fiancé, who was on his way back up the hill, came within earshot.

'They were his sister's. She and her husband were killed in a plane crash. He's their guardian.'

'Is he married?'

'No.'

'And you're just the children's nanny?'

'That's what I'm being paid for.' Sophy was filled with a spirit of mischief as she smiled with closed eyes and an expression of ecstatic bliss. 'Mind you, the perks of the job are out of this world.'

'I'm sure they are,' said Catherine tartly.

Sophy opened her eyes. 'Here comes Albert.'

'His name is Alaric,' snapped Catherine, and Sophy felt that the last few minutes had wiped out the years when Catherine had looked straight through her. Sophy had never been introduced to Alaric, who came from Edinburgh, but Cress had talked about Catherine's latest. He had been to dinner parties with Cress and Robin, and now when Catherine said that this was Cressida's sister he looked surprised.

'I didn't know Cressida had a sister.' He was stockily built and panting slightly from the exertion of climbing the hill, but he added admiringly, 'I can see why she keeps quiet about you!'

For the first time somebody thought that Sophy would be sexy competition for Cress, and that made her really laugh. So did Gavin, coming up with Felicity under one arm and dumping her at Sophy's feet and saying, 'Explain the rules of the game to this one.'

Felicity wailed, 'He smashed Hulk!' 'He' was the small boy with the 'sixer' whom she had attempted to knock flat, and who was still with them.

'That's Hulk's hard luck,' said Sophy, watching a tear trickle down Felicity's cheek that went very well with the catch in her voice.

'P-poor Hulk!'

'You can have my sixer,' offered the besotted small boy. 'It's a sevener now,' and Felicity turned to him with quivering lips.

'Any more trouble from you,' Gavin informed her, 'and you're back in the car!'

Felicity hiccuped, took the 'sevener', and went trotting off with the small boy. Charles had taken no notice at all of Felicity's dramatics, he was sending his egg down for a second run, and Gavin raised a quizzical eyebrow. 'I notice that she only slugs the boys. Does this mean I'm raising a man-hater?'

Sophy laughed, 'I shouldn't think you'll have any trouble that way. Look at her!' Felicity was dancing down the hill now, all smiles, her dark curls flying. 'The belle of the egg rolling!'

'She doesn't get my nomination,' said Gavin quietly, and he looked at Sophy and she could only see him. Everybody else seemed to melt into shadows, and she blushed, warmed to the heart.

Nothing could have dimmed the brightness of that hour. Catherine angled for Gavin's attention, being very gay and animated, and Sophy thought it was so obvious it was ridiculous. Nearly as absurd as Alaric trying to chat her up. When Catherine noticed that she gave up and led Alaric away. 'He's in line as husband number three,' Sophy murmured.

'Poor chap,' said Gavin.

'Don't you think she's fascinating?'

'No.' She clapped a hand over her mouth, to stop laughing, but she thought that there was something of Judith in Catherine.

She and Gavin sat down on the soft green grass and other friends and neighbours strolled over to them. Even some of the children remarked on the change in Sophy. 'You look terrific,' she was told, and, 'I like your jumper.' The adults controlled their surprise, mostly confining themselves to, 'You're looking well,' but they all wanted to meet Gavin.

He chatted and charmed, and Sophy was filled with pride. He was a super man, and for this hour he was hers. On their way home they would all be talking about Sophy Wade's arrival here with Gavin Tighe. She explained to him about Mrs Greenhaugh. 'I told my family I was working for her and they didn't ask me any more. They will today, though. I'm supposed to be taking the twins home for lunch. Will you——?'

'Thank you,' he said promptly, 'I'd like to,' and in

her present buoyant mood that was another little triumph.

'Cressida and Robin may be there,' she said. 'Cress said maybe. They met you at the business men's do when you gave a speech at the town hall here last month.'

Gavin didn't ask any questions, he just nodded, and Sophy went on handing out eggs, collecting cracked ones, talking to friends, while the sun shone in a clear blue sky. Perhaps it should have been a warning when Felicity announced dolefully, 'Your heart's smashed,' but it was just another egg, and Sophy dropped it into the bag with the rest.

They didn't all go to Sophy's home for lunch. Charles and Felicity had joined up with three brothers whose mother invited them back to her house for the afternoon. Sophy thought they would have more fun there, the Robinsons kept open house, and Charles and Felicity were clamouring to go with them. They all walked back to the car park together, where the twins clambered into the back of the Robinsons' Volvo Estate waving goodbye, until six o'clock when they were to be collected.

'Jack's head of the woodwork department at the Poly,' said Sophy, watching the car go. 'They're a super family.'

'Where now?' asked Gavin, at the wheel of his own car with Sophy beside him.

'My home, I suppose,' she said. She would rather have gone with the twins, the Robinsons' household was warm and bustling and she didn't really want to go home. Best of all she would have liked to clear off with Gavin for the hours between now and six o'clock, and seen nobody else at all. But he was driving towards the street where she lived, and she pulled down the sun visor to get a glimpse of her reflection in the little mirror.

She did look different. She was different. As though she had been in deep-freeze until she came close to Gavin and now she was warm and alive. She pushed her fingers slowly through her hair, lifting it, fluffing it, and ran a tongue tip over her lips. 'My mother's beautiful,' she told him. 'So is my sister,' and he smiled down at her.

'Stop fishing,' he said.

I am beautiful, she thought, and I don't need the words because every time you smile at me I know that. 'Just mentioning it,' she shrugged.

At the end of the street she started to direct him, and as the Mercedes turned into the drive of the Wade household she saw Cressida at the window. Before they were out of the car Cress was out of the door, in a flash of kingfisher blue silk dress, with her mother just behind her. They both had a startled look. Gavin and Sophy climbed out of the door and Sara and Cressida smiled twitchily, making little gestures of confusion.

'Where are the children?' Sara asked.

'We met the Robinsons in the park,' Sophy explained, 'and Mary asked them back. They've ganged up with the gang.'

'What's all this about?' Cress was half laughing, eyeing Gavin.

'This is——' Sophy began, and Cress's silvery voice swept over hers.

'I know who this is, but why didn't you *tell* us who you were working for?'

Somebody had phoned. Probably Catherine. 'You didn't ask,' said Sophy. 'Nobody wanted any details.'

Her mother said, 'Well, I haven't met you, have I?' and held out a small white hand which Gavin took with grave courtesy.

'I've been looking forward to meeting you,' he said

in his deep sexy voice, 'Sophy has told me so much about you.'

She didn't think she had. Not after that first night when she had babbled after the sleepwalking. But her mother's cool pale cheeks flushed and Sara Wade seemed temporarily at a loss as she led the way back into the house.

Sophy's father and Cress's husband were in the drawing room. Gavin Tighe was surprise enough, Sophy felt, and her father did not like surprises. But the change in Sophy herself added to the shock, so that her father almost glared at her for a moment. Robin gulped, then said heartily without stopping to choose his words, 'Well, hello, you're looking well on it!'

Cress gave him a sharp look and introduced Gavin to her father. 'Sophy didn't mention it, but this is the man she's working for. No wonder she looks a bit brighter these days!' Cress's smile was for Gavin. 'We have met before.' She was expecting him to remember. 'Did Sophy remind you? Last month?'

'But of course,' said Gavin.

'Sophy was hiding behind the potted plants and we couldn't get her out,' Cress pealed with merriment, 'because she'd tipped all the wine into her lap. Sophy has two left hands, you know.'

'I didn't know.' His eyes met Sophy's. 'And I'd have said that Sophy's anatomy was exactly right.' It was as though he touched her with hands that knew her every curve and hollow, every inch of skin and hair, right down to the bone.

She felt his touch and she felt her breasts tighten and she pretended to laugh, 'Not now I don't have two left hands!' This would amuse Gavin if it didn't amuse anyone else, and she picked up a Georgian decanter that was her mother's pride and joy, hearing Sara

Wade's sharp gasp. 'This is pretty, isn't it?' she said to Gavin, showing it to him as casually as though it was seconds from the market. 'You've got a matching pair very like it, haven't you?'

'Yes,' he said, and Sophy relented her teasing, reassuring her mother,

'I won't drop it. I'm wearing my contact lenses, so I can see what I'm about these days.'

'Can you?' asked Cress on a doubting note, and Sara waited until Sophy had put down the decanter, then said that lunch was ready to serve and perhaps Sophy would help her dish up.

Cress didn't go into the kitchen. She offered Gavin a drink and a chair as Sophy followed her mother, and once in the kitchen Sara demanded, 'How did this happen? How did you get this job?'

'It was advertised,' said Sophy, and that was the truth.

The meal Sara Wade had intended to set before Sophy and her two younger charges had been plain and simple, leg of lamb with peas and minted potatoes followed by apple pie. But when Cressida rang about an hour ago and told her mother that a man who was worth a million would probably be turning up too, and that she and Rob were coming over to find out what was going on, Sara had raided the deep-freeze for boeuf Stroganoff, and Gilbert had brought out a couple of bottles of good red wine. Sophy's visit, that nobody had intended putting themselves out for, had thrown her parents and her sister into almost panicky confusion.

Sara began stirring in the sour cream, still puzzled. 'Why didn't you say that Mrs Greenhaugh was just the housekeeper?' she asked.

'Are you sure I didn't? It could be you weren't listening. That's happened before.' Sophy was smiling, and Sara said indignantly, 'Of course I'm sure!'

Jokes were usually at Sophy's expense. She never laughed at the rest of the family, and the rest of the family never took much notice what Sophy was telling them. But today the awkward tongue-tied girl was a bright alert young woman, graceful and glowing, and with a model's figure. Something quite extraordinary had happened to Sophy these last three weeks.

The meal turned into a special event. Gilbert Wade drank several glasses of wine, and enjoyed having a guest of the mental calibre of Gavin Tighe at his table; and Sophy caught her father's astonished eyes on her several times when she gave an opinion or joked, or just talked as much as Cress, because she never had before.

Cress had always been the witty one, the centre of attention, but today, for the first time, Sophy felt her sister's equal, and after the meal when Sophy went up to her old room to collect her cassette player Cress went with her. As Sophy opened a drawer in a chest of drawers Cress sat on the bed and asked, 'Did you know you were going to work for him when we went to that dance?'

'I hadn't had the interview then,' said Sophy.

'But you knew you might and you never said a word—I'd never have believed you could be so sly!' Cress shivered deliciously. 'But wow, isn't he a gorgeous hulk?' She was lying back now, watching Sophy through slitted eyes. 'And he's certainly made a woman of you. What's he like as a lover?'

It was as though Sophy knew. As though she had lain naked in his arms, been taken passionately, savagely. Not even with tenderness. Like a tiger making love. Her face flamed, and Cress began to laugh.

'Was it rape? Don't tell me you went willingly? I'll bet you did, though, after the first few minutes.'

Sophy stood silent and her whole body seemed to be

burning. She would be a tiger herself, as soon as Gavin really touched her, and Cress was still laughing. 'I suppose you were a virgin? Not even Peter?' She waited a moment. 'No? Well, from the looks of you you've had an in-depth crash course. But don't get hooked on it with him, because he may be enjoying you now, but he'll send you packing when the job's over. I mean, I wouldn't like you to come back here and spend the rest of your life waiting for another Gavin Tighe . . .'

CHAPTER SIX

CRESSIDA was jealous. Sophy could never have imagined that happening in a million years, and anyway, Cress was wrong, Gavin was not Sophy's lover. She said shortly, 'Her name's Judith Gretton, Gavin's girl.'

'Which proves my point,' drawled Cressida. 'You're a very passing fancy. He's just playing with you.'

Sophy hadn't needed Cress to spell out that there was no future for her with Gavin, but until now the day had been so good that she could have wept at her sister's cruelty. Cress was being cruel, inflicting deliberate pain, and as well as tears, anger welled in Sophy.

She stood very tall, arms folded, smiling down at Cressida. 'I know it's a game,' she said sweetly, 'but wasn't I lucky finding a master player who knows all the moves? Does Rob? Could be I've learned more in my crash course than you have in years.'

Cressida stiffened, jerking herself upright, almost spitting out the words, 'You always were a fool!'

'I know I was,' said Sophy, 'and it wasn't much fun, I wasted a lot of time.' She put on the blissful expression that had shocked Catherine on the hill in the park. 'But since I went away I've hardly wasted a night.'

Cressida gasped and Sophy went on, 'Funny really. Everybody thinking I was frigid and frumpy, when what I was really meant to be was a very sexy lady.'

Cressida would believe that now. The gauche girl who had always been a foil had suddenly developed an innate sensuality that was like star quality in an actress, and Cressida envied the lovemaking that had ignited Sophy. Thinking of Gavin Tighe as a lover had been turning her on all through lunch. It was sickening that Sophy had him, even if it was only for a few more weeks, when he was so much richer and sexier than any man Cress had ever had. She got off the bed and snapped, 'I think you've gone off your head!'

'Do you?' Sophy seemed to consider that. 'Well, it's a marvellous sort of madness.'

'Peter won't want you afterwards.' Cressida said the first thing she could think of, and Sophy laughed a little.

'What's the difference? He didn't want me before.' She opened the bottom drawer of the chest of drawers and the magazine was still there. 'I think Peter read the article,' she said. 'It's a crazy world, isn't it, the way things work out?'

Cress told her again that she was a fool, and then flounced out of the room, and Sophy let out a long shuddering sigh. She had lied her way through that, confirming what Cress had taken for granted, that Sophy's relationship with Gavin was physical when in fact he had hardly touched her. He had brought her to womanhood with words and actions that could have been summed up as kindness, although she had been there for the taking from that first night.

The message was in her lips, her eyes. Her whole body was begging, 'Love me!' She knew it. Anybody could see it, and he must see it too, and maybe he would. Take her, not love her. Love was a commitment, and there would never be that.

Sophy sat down on the edge of the bed, hunching her shoulders, her head bowed. If Cress had not said those things Sophy would never have thought beyond the night. She knew it couldn't last, but she would have responded passionately. She wouldn't have thought about afterwards if Cress hadn't said, 'I wouldn't like you to spend the rest of your life waiting for another Gavin Tighe.'

Dreams faded. For years she had dreamed of Peter, but memories of Gavin could stay aching inside her for ever. 'Don't get hooked on it with him,' Cress had said and she would, she *would*. If she let him make love to her it would be like food and drink for which her whole system craved, and she might see him again, during other school holidays, but she would never mean more to him than a few nights' stand. 'No,' she said on a whisper that was a sob, and stayed where she was, sitting rigid on the side of the bed, before she was ready to go downstairs and face them all.

Then she collected half a dozen cassettes. There was nothing else she wanted to take away with her. Some clothes and shoes were still in the wardrobe, but they were a style she would probably never wear again. Something for Oxfam, she thought. She almost took down the map on the wall—but perhaps the one the children had made for themselves was better. 'Here be tygers,' she read, and smiled wryly. Tigers devour, and being gobbled up might have been exquisite pain, but there wasn't much future in it.

Her mother opened the door, asking, 'What are you doing up here?'

'Fetching these.' She held up a cassette and Sara said,

'You've been ages. Cress and Rob have had to go, they're expecting company.' She came into the room, looking up at her tall lovely daughter, still with an air of faint bewilderment. 'What's the house like?' she asked.

'Not all that imposing outside.' Sophy had always

known that her mother put great value on material things, and she found herself humouring her. 'It's the old family home. There was a mill there once but it was all in a small way until Gavin's day. Inside there are some beautiful things you'd love.' She began to describe them, and Sara Wade realised that Sophy's knowledge of antiques was probably as good as Cressida's. Behind Sophy's wide eyes, which had always looked blank and stupid to her mother, there had to be a retentive mind.

'He has two other homes,' said Sophy. 'A penthouse flat on Cannock Chase, in the Midlands where the second factory is, and an old manor house in Dorset which is run as a conference centre. He's very rich and very successful.'

Her mother was impressed, and Sophy, having started talking about Gavin, just went on. 'He's tough, of course—well, he has to be, but the children adore him; and so do the housekeeper and her husband who've known him all his life. He's been very kind to me too. The first night I got there, I suppose I must have been homesick or something, because I found myself sleepwalking in the middle of the night. You remember how I used to?' Her mother nodded and Sophy grimaced, 'Well, imagine, a sleepwalking nanny! But he was very understanding about it, and that won't happen again because I am very happy there. I love the twins, they're real characters, both of them, and the Greenhaughs are like—well, like a second family to me.'

Sara Wade was listening now, to every word. She had always considered herself a good mother, but in a few weeks this other 'family' had given Sophy a confidence that transfigured her. Most of it had to be the man, of course, and all Sara could do was offer advice. She said gently, 'He's very attractive. He's a hundred per cent man and I can understand you being attracted to him, but don't lose your head completely.'

Nor my heart, thought Sophy. 'No,' she said.

'Peter hasn't been in touch?'

'No. Cress tells me he's going around with Anne Marie again.'

'He should have been here today,' said Sara Wade, looking Sophy up and down, and when Sophy laughed so did she, although she soon became serious again. 'You will be coming home in a fortnight?'

'Of course.' Sophy grinned. 'By then the lawn *will* need cutting! Tell Nick I said to get out there.'

It was a joke, not a rebuke, but Sara Wade felt it as a rebuke and protested, 'I wasn't thinking about the garden, I was thinking about you. Will you be seeing Gavin again afterwards?'

'I doubt it.' Sophy made that sound casual, although it turned her heart to lead. 'Don't worry,' she said, 'I know he's not for me.' She laughed again, 'Everybody's telling me. Cress has just finished warning me. Now you. Will my father be having a few words before we leave?'

'I shouldn't think so.' Sophy was still joking and Sara smiled wryly, 'But of course Cress is concerned about you.'

Cress is a bitch, thought Sophy, who wants me back where I was, as I was. Cress is spitting mad. But her mother's concern was based on love and Sophy, surprised and touched, hugged her and reassured her cheerfully, 'No danger. I'm having a lovely holiday, and that's all it is.'

They collected the twins at six o'clock, from a rambling old house backing on to the grounds of the college, where both Jack Robinson and Sophy's father worked. Sophy got on very well with the Robinsons, she looked after the children sometimes, giving Mary and Jack an evening out.

Lester, Joe and Harvey, were just finishing tea, with Felicity and Charles, around the big scrubbed-topped kitchen table, and they all greeted Sophy and Gavin with wide grins. 'Have we *got* to come yet?' asked Felicity, her grin fading.

'In five minutes,' said Gavin, and Charles looked up at the clock on the wall and asked, 'Then can I have another flapjack, please?'

It was nearer half an hour before they left, because Jack took Gavin into his workroom to see an old sea chest he was restoring, and Sophy gave Mary a hand clearing the table.

'I can't get over the way you look,' said Mary, for the third time, as Sophy hung mugs on the dresser. Mary wasn't jealous, although she was plump and freckled herself and only beautiful in the eyes of her family. And when she asked, 'Are you still seeing Peter Fisher?' that was friendly interest.

'No,' said Sophy, and might have gone on to add something if Gavin and Jack hadn't walked back into the kitchen. So then the twins had to say their goodbyes. Mary and the three Robinson boys were invited over to Witherstone, and the Robinsons came out into the road to wave as the car drew away.

Sophy was beginning to feel tired. All the way home the twins chattered about the games they had played, and what they had had for lunch and tea, and what they would do on Tuesday week when Lester and Joe and Harvey came to their home. Sophy answered when she had to. Sometimes Gavin did, but most of the time he left it to Sophy and she found herself replying abstractedly and being sharply rebuked, 'You don't mean *yes*, you mean *no!*'

'Oh, sorry, do I? Yes, of course—no.'

'No what?' Charles wasn't letting her get away with that, but Gavin said,

'No, she didn't want to stay there and not come back with us,' and then Sophy whirled round, all contrition. 'I wasn't listening properly.'

It would have been grim, being left behind. She was so glad she was going back to the Old Mill House, where Mrs Greenhaugh and Tom were waiting for them.

As soon as they were in the house the twins started to relive their day all over again, shouting each other down, and Mrs Greenhaugh, looking a little flushed, said it sounded as though they'd had a champion time; and Sophy said oh, they had, but now it was bedtime, and without further ado marched them upstairs.

She got them undressed and bathed and into bed, and got away with a shortened bedtime story because when they slid between the sheets they collapsed. Their eyes were glassy with fatigue, and they lay motionless but determined to hear every last word, until she concluded with, 'And that's all for tonight,' when they both gave a happy little sigh and were fast asleep.

Downstairs there was no sign of Gavin. There had been phone calls for him. Nothing urgent enough to warrant chasing him up the callers had said, but some that he was chasing up because he had gone into the study with the numbers and was still there. Sophy wondered if Judith had rung and if he was talking to her all this time, and what he was telling her.

Mrs Greenhaugh sneezed again, she was sitting with a shawl around her, and Sophy took a good look at her. 'You *do* have a cold!' she accused.

'I've been telling her that all day,' said Tom.

'You need to go to bed with a hot drink,' said Sophy. 'Two aspirins and a slug of whisky. I know all about it,' she laughed, 'my father takes great care of his health, one sneeze and he's prostrate. But it's just as silly to stagger on when you can easily have an early night and make a fuss of yourself.'

'I've been telling her that all day too,' said Tom.

'You're turning into a right pushy little madam,' said Mrs Greenhaugh, but she was getting out of her chair. 'I've got the aspirins,' she said. 'Tom can bring up the whisky.' At the bottom of the stairs she asked, 'Did you see your folk?'

'Not my brother. He was out somewhere. The rest of the family thought I looked very well.'

'Well, you do,' said Mrs Greenhaugh, and went up the stairs quite slowly, so that Sophy standing at the bottom bit her lip, and thought that Mrs Greenhaugh looked quite old, and felt as distressed as though she had lived here and known this woman all her life.

Tom poured out whisky for his wife, himself and Sophy, and said he was glad Sophy had persuaded Ada to have an early night. 'Mr Gavin would have packed her off,' he said, 'but he'd got his mind on the business. One of those calls was from Saudi Arabia.'

'Fancy that!' Sophy murmured.

'She will keep on her feet,' said Tom. 'Nobody can do anything like she can, but she thinks a lot of you.'

'I think a lot of her,' said Sophy, flattered that Mrs Greenhaugh seemed to have waited until she was back before giving up and going to bed.

Tom handed her a glass, one part whisky, two parts water, and said, 'I'd take this upstairs if I was you. You've had a busy day. You're starting to look all in yourself.'

Sophy was feeling the strain of putting on a brave face ever since her scene with Cress. She had begun to think of this house as her home, but when she was alone in the nursery tonight loneliness closed in on her just as it had that first night. She busied herself, getting the children's clothes ready for tomorrow, washing her hair, taking a long slow bath, and finally sitting down with a thriller that she had found on the bookshelves downstairs. It was a well-known best-seller, but although she kept turning over the pages she wasn't taking in much of the story.

She had saved the glass of whisky to drink to help herself sleep, and when it was bedtime she gulped it down and set the empty glass on the table, then sat with the book on her knee waiting for drowsiness to overcome misery. She didn't think it was going to work, but it did slow down her reactions, so that when the door opened it took her a moment to wipe the sadness from her face.

'Coming down for a nightcap?' asked Gavin.

He was still fully dressed. Sophy was in her dressing gown, and she nodded towards the empty glass, 'I've just had one.' It was almost eleven and his eyes looked tired. She knew he had come from his desk, looking for her, and she was pleased that he wanted her company for this last half hour. She got up and said, 'I'm not a secret drinker, I've been keeping this for a nightcap. Tom gave it to me when he was dosing Mrs G. for her cold, hours ago.'

'Come and have another,' said Gavin, and led the way downstairs again into the drawing room.

The heavy silk kimono, with its scarlet peony, that she had borrowed the first morning she came here, still hung behind that bathroom door. She still didn't know who it belonged to, still thought it was probably Judith's, and she wished now that she had bought herself something more exotic than the schoolgirlish navy blue dressing gown she had brought from home. She had never been downstairs in this before.

The remains of a log fire burned in the big white

marble fireplace and Gavin poured two measures of whisky, adding a splash of soda to his, ginger ale to Sophy's. They had sipped drinks together like this before, it was almost a cosy domestic scene, but until tonight she had never been uneasy with him.

She was sitting on the chesterfield, as she usually did. He placed her glass on a low table in front of her, took the other end of the sofa and said, 'It didn't go as you planned?'

'What didn't?'

'Today.'

She didn't understand. Gavin sat back, long legs crossed, watching her. 'I didn't plan today,' she said. 'Except to amuse the children, to have lunch at home.' But when he said, 'Tell me about Peter,' she supposed she had, in a way, imagined meeting Peter again and astounding him with her changed appearance and her new assertiveness.

She hadn't met Peter and it hadn't mattered. She said, 'You heard Mary asking me about him?' He nodded. 'Well, there isn't much to tell.' She took a gulp of whisky, then realised she had had enough and put the glass back on the table and said, 'Before I came here I was going around with a man called Peter, but it petered out.' She hadn't meant that as a pun, but when she heard it she smiled.

Gavin didn't smile. 'Just like that?' he said.

'Nearly.' One moment she had believed that Peter loved her. Then she overheard a few words being spoken and knew that he didn't. 'Nearly as suddenly as that,' she said. 'I think you did it.'

Now it was his turn to look blank and ask, 'What?'

Sophy sat back herself, her hands limp in her lap, speaking slowly and deliberately. 'Peter admires you tremendously. You are the man he would like to be. You met him at that do as well as Cress and Rob and about sixty others—Peter Fisher, tallish, works for Swarbrick Engineering, Preston, but one of his ambitions is to work for Tighe Industries.'

She couldn't tell if Gavin remembered. She couldn't tell anything from his face, but she went on talking. 'You gave an interview in a women's magazine, it came out last month. And you said that no man who wanted to succeed should get himself lumbered with a quiet woman. Well, that was me, wasn't it?' She gave a small shrug of self-disparagement. 'I mean I was so quiet no one thought there was anything going on in my head. And Peter read it, I reckon, and thought, fair enough, the words of the master.'

'This isn't for real?' Gavin said incredulously. 'Nobody could have taken that rubbish seriously!'

'They could, you know. Did you never wonder why my name wasn't on the list?'

'The list?'

'The ones who phoned up about the job. The list Mrs Greenhaugh lost.'

'That the twins probably disposed of.'

'Did they?' It was the first she had heard of that, but when he explained, 'Anything to confuse the nanny issue' she considered it likely.

'Yes,' she said. 'Well, I never saw an advertisement, I didn't know you were looking for a nanny. What I came for was to tell you you were wrong about quiet women. I'd just heard Peter telling my brother he intended to go places like you, and I wasn't going to be much help, dragging along behind him.' The whisky, and all that had happened to her since, dulled the knife-edge of that memory, but it was still sharp enough to make her wince. 'I went spare that morning, I cleared off without telling anyone where I was going.' She took another couple of gulps from her glass and stared down into the amber liquid. 'I think I only came to my senses after I dived into the lake. There's nothing like cold water.'

'So they say,' said Gavin.

'I'm not a drag now, am I?' and Sophy raised woebegone eyes.

'No.'

'What do you think Peter would think of me now?'

'You're asking what I think?'

'I just did.'

'I think you should forget him.' He drew her towards him, so that her head fell against his shoulder. He stroked her hair and then her cheek, and his touch under her hair was like sweet fire, her head fell lower and he brushed the nape of her neck with his lips and she felt the impact pierce her whole body in pure throbbing sensation.

'I could make you forget him.' Gavin's voice was husky, and if his mouth closed on hers nothing would reach her except through him. He could make her forget her own name for as long as he made love to her. For tonight. For two weeks. But after that how would she go about forgetting him?

Cress was right. Her mother was right. Her mind cleared, as it had in the cold water of the lake, and a rasping sob was torn from her throat. 'No, please, no—oh, please don't!' and he said quietly, 'You don't want to forget him?'

Peter? She *had* forgotten. But Peter could be in her life this time next month, which was more than Gavin would be. Peter was an excuse that Gavin might understand and accept. She babbled, 'It's always been Peter, I've always been in love with him. I think you're terribly attractive and I'm sure you can have almost any woman you meet, but——'

'But not you?' He was smiling at her. 'I believe you. There's no need to look so desperate.'

It was no big thing to him. He hadn't taken offence and he didn't give a damn. By asking he had shown her she was desirable, and she would always remember that, but so were others who wouldn't say no. She took the glass in both hands and finished her drink, then asked, 'Could I have another?'

'You could, of course, if you're sure you want one. But I think you have probably had enough.' Gavin spoke with amusement and she said,

'You're right, of course. Goodnight, then. It was a good day.'

'I thought so too. Goodnight.'

Sophy made herself walk out of the room. It was hard, because every step hurt. She wanted to run back to him and if he had even said her name she would have done. But he didn't, and when she turned at the door he wasn't even looking her way, so she went on up the stairs.

Of course she had regrets, bitter regrets that would probably keep her aching and awake. Cress would smile if she knew that Sophy was alone tonight because of what Cress had said; and if Cress knew that this was the first night when Sophy need not have been alone she would go into hysterics. 'You always were a fool,' Cress had said, and through that restless lonely night, when she could have been in Gavin's arms, Sophy agreed with her . . .

But next morning she was proud of herself. She lay for a few moments, when she woke, thinking how sensible she had been. It would have been absolute madness. This morning she would have been wandering around in a fool's paradise, and then out into the cold like poor old Eve thrown out of Eden. Oh, it was much better and safer to wake here, in her own bed; and there wouldn't be another chance to wreck her life now Gavin believed that she loved Peter and was faithful to Peter, and hoping that Peter would approve of her new and sexy self and take her on again.

She got out of bed, and reached for her dressing gown. 'Peter won't want you after this,' Cress had taunted, and Sophy thought, You've been wrong about a lot of things, my know-all sister. When I come home again there'll be changes, and one of the changes will be the way men look at me, and one of the men will be Peter.

That thought cheered her. She smiled at herself in the dressing table mirror as she passed. But there might never be another chance with Gavin, and her smile was suddenly shaky so that she had to bite her underlip to steady it.

The children were still sleeping and she went down to the kitchen to get herself a cup of coffee. After that perhaps she could start the day as calmly as she hoped to go on. Mrs Greenhaugh was always downstairs by now, but this morning Tom was in the kitchen alone, and when Sophy walked in he said, 'I was in two minds whether to call you. I don't think she should be getting up, I don't like the looks of her.'

Mrs Greenhaugh was not a pretty sight. She looked flushed and furious, and when Sophy arrived by her bed she said, 'You know where I've got this from, don't you? It's that Agnes, this is. Blowing her germs all over everybody!'

On Friday Mrs Greenhaugh had been very sympathetic towards Agnes, who had been under the weather, insisting that she go home. Sophy had driven her home, to her daughter's house, to be told there was a lot of it about. Now Mrs Greenhaugh had the sweats and shivers herself, and was blaming Agnes for the frustration of her condition.

'We'll be lucky if we don't all go down with it,' she

said darkly. 'Mr Gavin's off to the Midlands for the week. Most likely he'll be taking it down there.'

'I shouldn't think it's the bubonic plague,' said Sophy with a smile and a sigh. She was sorry for Mrs Greenhaugh, but she was sure it was just gastric 'flu, for which a day or two in bed was the best cure. She could deal with that. It was hearing that Gavin would be away for the rest of the week that made her sigh. It shouldn't, she had to get used to being without him. And certainly it shouldn't surprise her, because of course he moved around, all over the country, all over the world. She said, 'We'll have the doctor in. Yes, we will,' as Mrs Greenhaugh started to protest.

'You'll need some help if I'm lying here,' said Mrs Greenhaugh mournfully.

'I can manage,' said Sophy. 'You know I can. And the twins will behave, you'll see.'

Mrs Greenhaugh settled back on her pillow. 'Only for a day or two,' she sighed.

The doctor, who looked like a thick-set ruddy-complexioned farmer in tweed jacket and cords, was reassuring. Nothing to worry about he said, leaving anti-biotic pills, but she had to keep warm and quiet with plenty of hot drinks, and she shouldn't count on getting up this side of the weekend. He also agreed that there was a lot of it about.

Gavin had waited to see the doctor, and afterwards he sat down at the breakfast table with Sophy and the twins. The twins were subdued. This was the first time they had known Mrs G. take to her bed, and they looked apprehensively at Sophy for signs of weakness in her. She realised that not even in nightmares could they imagine anything happening to Gavin. He was the rock on which their lives were built, and she envied them their claim to him.

He reassured them about Mrs G. So long as they

did everything Sophy and Tom told them they would be helping her get well again. He would be phoning each night, and he was relying on them. They nodded, their eyes shining with good intentions, and Sophy wondered how long that would last.

'If you find you need any help,' he told her, as she walked with him to the garage and his car, 'ring my secretary. The number's on the pad on my desk. She'll get you a nurse if it's necessary and she can always get in touch with me. Tom can get you domestic help locally.'

'I'll cope,' said Sophy. 'There isn't an army to feed.'

Mrs Greenhaugh didn't seem to want the size of the staff increasing. The other Tighe homes might be different, but here Mrs Greenhaugh managed happily with Agnes doing part-time, as though she guarded the house from outsiders. Gavin Tighe might be a wealthy man, but his life style here was unostentatious.

It wouldn't be if he married Judith, thought Sophy. She would want more than the Greenhaughs taking her orders. There'd be some changes made if Judith took charge here, but I don't believe he will marry her or he surely wouldn't have made a pass at me last night.

He said goodbye, warned the children again and told Sophy to look after herself as well as everybody else, lifted Felicity up for a kiss and ruffled Charles' hair; and then drove away in the Mercedes, a devastating, sophisticated man of the world.

Sophy thought, he has the looks, the brains, the money. I'd have to be a very simple soul to think he doesn't have the women too. Of course he could plan to marry Judith and because I seemed to be there for the taking take me, and count it no more than lingering over a palatable bottle of wine.

She shivered, and Charles tugged her hand and queried anxiously, 'You're not getting sick, are you?'

'No,' she smiled then, 'I'm fit as a fiddle.' But she did feel sick, although it was nothing like Mrs G.'s ailment.

Gavin's departure left an emptiness. Even on the nights he hadn't come home Sophy had known that he would be here next day, but now the days stretched ahead, and although there were only six of them until Saturday night it seemed a very long time.

She was glad of the extra work. The twins were hardly any trouble, partly because they thought that Mrs G. might have chicken-pox-without-the-spots, brought in by them from the school epidemic. Sophy appointed Felicity nurse in charge of medication, sitting beside the bed to check that the patient swallowed her pills. Mrs G. couldn't make a fuss in front of the twins, it would have been bad for her image, so she took her medicine, but not with a very good grace.

And she drank the hot drinks, and Sophy consulted her on every household move, because Mrs G. had a system and if she thought it was going haywire she would have been getting up too soon or lying in bed worrying.

Gavin phoned on Monday night, and Felicity got to the phone first and said, 'Yes, hello, yes,' listened for a moment and then offered Sophy the phone. 'He wants to talk to you, but it's only Uncle Gavin.'

The call to Sophy was brief, just checking that she was coping, and afterwards he talked to the twins for another five minutes, but the sound of his voice sent her senses singing with delight. Like the aftershave. She unstoppered that in the bathroom and sniffed it, and it brought Gavin close for a moment. He was away, the house was empty, although she loved being with the twins and looking after them all, but it was his house, so that everything she touched and everywhere she went had his stamp on it.

Wednesday was Mrs Greenhaugh's day for the bedrooms, and Sophy went into Gavin's bedroom for the first time since she had sleep-walked that first night, when she had been left with what seemed like a vivid recollection of the room, although she had been dazed out of her mind. Tom was looking after the children, who were 'helping' him in the garden, and Sophy had gone briskly through the room next door.

This was where the twins said Judith slept when she stayed. So far as Sophy knew she hadn't stayed overnight in the last few weeks, but this was well away from the nursery and her own room, so she couldn't know for sure. The bed was made up and the sheets were fresh. It was ready if it was needed. The thick rose-coloured carpet hadn't a mark on it, and Sophy had flicked a duster over the dressing table with an expression of distaste. She could imagine Judith sitting here, brushing her glorious hair, waiting for Gavin. Or going to him, looking absolutely ravishing.

She got out of that room and went into Gavin's, and it was how she remembered except that the bed was tidy. The night she was in here the sheets had been thrown back because he had jumped out, hearing her fall down the three little steps outside. Sophy was changing sheets today, and she turned down the dark brown linen coverlet.

It she hadn't panicked she might have slept in this bed on Sunday night. Or perhaps not slept but lain here against the hard nakedness of his body, his arms around her. She picked up the pillow to slip off the pillowcase and held it close, burying her face in it, going so weak at the knees that she had to sit down on the bed.

Perhaps she hadn't been so smart. Cress was right, of course, Sophy's days here were numbered, but maybe she should have taken what she could in the little time she had. She closed her eyes, still hugging the pillow, and desire rose inside her, primitive and painful, a force of nature taking her by storm so that she moaned and then almost flung the pillow away.

Damn Cress. What had any of it to do with her? Sophy gathered up the bedclothes and got out of the room. She knew what the price would be but she wanted Gavin so much that nothing else mattered. If I get another chance, she vowed, I won't say no. I won't say anything. But next time, if there is a next time, he won't see me running away ...

Mrs Greenhaugh continued to improve and nobody else went down. Agnes came back on Thursday, but kept out of Mrs G.'s room, although as she said plaintively to Sophy and Tom, 'How does she know she got it off me?' The twins had informed her on that point as soon as she put her head round the door. 'Mine was only a cold, I didn't have no aching bones with mine. How's she getting on?'

'She's doing all right,' said Sophy, and Mrs G. was soon eating her meals, giving her orders, and determined to be downstairs for Gavin's homecoming on Saturday.

He phoned each night, had a few words with Sophy and rather more with the twins, and listening to him always liquified Sophy's bones so that she usually finished sitting on the bottom of the stairs waiting for the twins to finish their conversation. They told him some hair-raising tales, all of which had a faint basis of fact, and the first day Sophy spoke to him afterwards and said, 'You are taking all this with a pinch of salt, aren't you?' and he had laughed. Afterwards she just told him that all was well, and on Friday she had added, 'We're missing you.'

She had a couple of calls from home that week. The first, on Monday night, was from Nick, who started with, 'What the hell is going on?' and before Sophy could draw breath, 'They tell me you're working for Gavin Tighe, of all folk!'

'They tell you right,' said Sophy.

'Why did you keep that dark?' Nick had been away for the weekend, returning to his flat after work on Monday and hearing from his mother about Sophy's arrival yesterday with the man who turned out to be employing her, not that Mrs Greenhaugh at all. What was more, he wouldn't have known his sister, said Sara Wade. An obvious exaggeration, but Sophy's new situation seemed to have brought her out of her shell with a vengeance, and Nick had immediately rung the number they had all had for three weeks and never used before and asked Sophy what was going on.

It was time for Gavin to phone, and Sophy said, 'We're expecting a call, I'll have to cut you off, but don't you worry about me, I'm loving the job and I couldn't be happier.'

'Who was that?' asked Felicity.

'My brother,' said Sophy, and Felicity pulled her *yeuk* face.

On Saturday morning Sophy got a call from her mother, who was showing more interest in how Sophy was feeling and what she was doing than ever before, and who seemed so relieved to hear that Gavin was away that Sophy hadn't the heart to add he was due back today. She wished she could have told her mother, just to hear the words, 'He'll be here tonight.' They sounded lovely, said over and over again to herself. They made her want to dance, like Felicity who had been skipping with excitement and watching the clock since breakfast.

'He brings them presents,' Mrs Greenhaugh explained, but it wasn't only the gifts they wanted. It was Gavin back. And so did Mrs Greenhaugh and Tom, and so did Sophy, although she would have died of embarrassment if Mrs G. had suspected the gift that Sophy wanted . . .

Mrs Greenhaugh was mistress in the kitchen again today, and the meal was to be a special welcome home supper for which the twins would be allowed to sit up. They laid the table in the little dining room, and when everything was ready Sophy changed out of her denim skirt and checked shirt and into a silk shirt in coral and matching silk jeans.

It was a new outfit, worn with bronze sandals, and she fixed her make-up and her hair, dabbed on plenty of perfume, and sat with the children in the drawing room, watching television. She had never felt happier. She didn't care about the future, she wouldn't think about it. Right now life was almost perfect, waiting and knowing that he would come. Anticipation fizzed inside her like champagne. When the children ran to him she would find it hard to stand still. She wanted to reach him and touch him so badly. But seeing him, smiling at him and speaking to him would be the next best thing, and later, when everyone was asleep, then . . .

She heard the car coming. The children jumped up from the floor in front of the television, where they had been lying full length, chins cupped in their hands, staring up at the screen. Charles pulled back the long velvet curtain and Sophy breathed deep and slow. She would stand up now and walk to the door with them to meet him.

'Oh, *she's* come!' said Felicity in long-suffering

tones, and Charles said hopefully, 'P'raps she won't stay.'

Sophy went to the window. The lights from the house made it bright as day, and Gavin was out of the car, and so was Judith. He was taking cases from the boot, one of them looked like a woman's. Judith had probably been with him all week and she was staying here now.

Sophy saw the white blur of her own reflected face on the dark pane of the window and stared at it to blot out the picture beyond. In her head she was screaming, over and over again, 'Oh, you fool, you fool, you *fool*!'

CHAPTER SEVEN

TODAY Sophy had hardly thought of Judith at all. She had let herself look forward to Gavin's homecoming as though he was coming home to her, and she was part of his household and his life. But Judith was the woman in his life. When they walked through the front door into the hall together it could have been a scene from a film: the tall dark striking man, the beautiful blonde woman, the children running towards them; Sophy was the outsider again, and it felt new and heartrending.

The children headed for Gavin, while Judith smiled sweetly. Then she saw Sophy and her eyes narrowed and over the babble of the children's voices she said, 'The air up here seems to be suiting you. You *have* blossomed out!'

'Thank you,' Sophy murmured.

Judith began to stroke Felicity's hair, making herself part of the group, and Felicity looked up startled. 'Now why should she thank me?' Judith smiled slantingly at Gavin. 'What could I have had to do with waking the sleeping beauty?'

Gavin looked at Sophy then. She was no surprise to him. He knew how she had changed since she came here. He smiled and asked her, 'Any problems?'

'None.' Except that she had wanted him to come home alone and put his arms around her like he did the night before he went away.

'Poor Mrs. G.,' Judith descended on her, 'it must have been beastly for you! You should have had a nurse in. Whatever made Nanny decide she could run the whole shoot? It must have been chaotic!'

'Everything was managed very nicely, thank you,' said Mrs Greenhaugh. 'Sophy looked after us all very well. Looked after everything and kept everything very nice. The meal's ready as soon as you are.'

The twins were clamouring for their presents, and when Gavin took up the cases they ran up the stairs beside him. Mrs Greenhaugh went back to the kitchen and Judith slipped out of a pearl-grey suede coat, supple as silk, held it towards Sophy and said curtly, 'Put this in the cloakroom.'

Sophy took the coat. She didn't mind hanging it up, although she knew she was being reminded of her status in this house. Judith came to the door of the cloakroom and said, 'Praise from Mrs G.! She's usually very fussy. You must be a super skivvy.'

'I do my best,' said Sophy.

'I'm sure you do.' Judith looked at her own reflection in the mirror over the handbasin, and then at Sophy. 'Only in this case, Nanny, your best isn't nearly good enough.'

I know that, thought Sophy. Do you think I can't see that? She watched Judith walk across the hall and go up the stairs. Perhaps to her room, which adjoined Gavin's. Perhaps to find them all, Gavin and the children, and watch the presents being unwrapped. Sophy went towards the kitchen, knowing that she must give no sign that Judith had read her right. That if Gavin had come back alone tonight she would have done her best to make him want to make love to her.

She could forget that now. From now on Judith would see that Sophy kept her distance from Gavin, but Judith need not worry. No girl looking like Judith need worry.

In the kitchen Mrs Greenhaugh was opening the oven door, and Sophy asked, 'Shall I lay another place, or will they eat alone?'

'I'm starting to feel a bit tired,' Mrs Greenhaugh decided. 'Tom and me'll have ours in here, but the children were promised.' The children would have been disappointed at being barred from the welcome-home meal, and that meant that Sophy had to take her place with them, although she would have been more comfortable with Tom and Ada. Judith had not been expected, but she was accepted without fuss, as a constant visitor.

'Does she have a job?' Sophy asked casually, and Mrs Greenhaugh shrugged.

'Her father's comfortably off. Not in as big a way as Mr Gavin, of course, there's few as are.' Sophy had to smile, Mrs G. sounded so smug about that. 'But he's got this advertising agency, and she's supposed to work for him, but she seems to go where she likes when she likes, and for the last six months that's usually been where Mr Gavin is.'

'It's serious, then?' Sophy tried to sound only mildly curious, and Mrs G. set a large shiny brown ovenware pot on the table and said, 'Oh, I think so.' She didn't seem enthusiastic, but she did seem fairly sure, and Sophy asked, 'Are you pleased about it?'

'If she suits him she'll have to suit us,' said Mrs Greenhaugh philosophically. 'She'll make him a fine-looking wife. He's had some good-looking girls, but I've got to admit she's——'

'That she is,' said Sophy, and Felicity came running into the kitchen, carrying a cardboard box with the lid off, which she put down on a chair.

'Will you help me put these on?' she asked Sophy. 'I don't want her to help me, I want you.'

'These' were a gipsy dress and kerchief, in green and red, and a small black velvet bolero. Gold medallions edged kerchief and bolero and there were bangles and chains, and Felicity, with her dark curls, was going to look like a picture-book Romany.

Judith must have walked in on the present opening, offered to help dress Felicity and had her offer refused, and although Sophy said, 'I hope you didn't give Judith any cheek,' she felt pleased that Felicity had come running to her.

'I said thank you,' said Felicity virtuously, 'but I had to show you and Mrs G.' She had her T-shirt over her head, and she wriggled out of it as Sophy tugged.

'You can tell my fortune,' said Mrs Greenhaugh, holding out the dress.

'I have to have everything on first.' Felicity had no doubts that this outfit carried its own powers, and when she was in it she would be able to do wonderful things. 'And Sophy's fortune,' she said, and Sophy, pressing press-studs and fixing the kerchief headdress. thought that she wanted no glimpse into her future.

Life was going to be better than before she came here. There was so much more she could do now. She could buy herself a small second-hand car, help in the shop maybe, go to auctions. Nobody was going to underrate her again. But she couldn't see happiness ahead, not real happiness. She hung the shining chains round Felicity's neck and slipped the bangles on to the thin childish arms and said, 'Now you're a real gipsy princess. And what's Charles?'

'He's got a kite,' said Felicity.

'If there's a wind tomorrow,' said Sophy, 'we'll go to the top of a hill and fly it.'

Felicity told their fortunes while they carried the first course into the small dining room. 'Am I going to win the pools?' asked Mrs G., who never did them. 'Oh *yes*,' said Felicity, and Tom came out of the little parlour to ask, 'What's my lucky number, then?'

'Seven,' said Felicity. Sophy asked anything she could think of in the spirit of the game and Felicity promised everything, dancing around the hall, until Judith and Charles started to come down the stairs and Felicity shrieked, 'Look at me, look at me, I'm a gipsy princess!' and Judith drawled, 'My goodness, we are over-excited!'

It was well past their bedtime, and perhaps Felicity was getting out of hand, and Sophy said 'All right now, steady down.' Felicity pouted and pirrouetted but then she shut up. 'Go and sit down at the table,' said Sophy and the children went into the dining room.

There was no one in the hall but Sophy. Gavin was probably following behind, because Judith glanced back up the empty staircase before she walked quickly over to Sophy and said very softly, 'Very good, but don't expect to be asked back next holidays, because by then I'll be choosing the nanny.'

Gavin came downstairs and Judith waited for him as Sophy turned for the dining room. Even with her back towards them she could imagine Judith's smile, and his, and see Judith slip her hand through Gavin's arm before they followed Sophy.

The meal was an ordeal. The casseroled chicken was succulent, but Judith wasn't hungry, and Gavin was called to the phone almost as soon as he sat down, and the children talked too much. Perhaps Sophy could have quietened them, but when she did the silence lay heavy. Judith picked at her food, looking bored, and watching the door for Gavin's return. It was Charles who asked, 'Did you go to Cannock with Uncle Gavin?' and Judith said, 'Yes.'

'It's nice, isn't it?' said Felicity. 'Not as nice as here, though,' she told Sophy. 'It's a flat there.' She went on to describe the luxury apartment, and Sophy found that as the pictures of the rooms came into her head she was peopling them with Gavin and Judith, talking, laughing. Making love. That made her nearly choke on a small chicken bone, and by the time she had been thumped on the back by Felicity, watched wearily by Judith, and managed to cough it out, the flat was forgotten by the twins.

They chattered on about other things and Sophy let them. Judith didn't say a word, and Sophy couldn't think of any bright topics of conversation, so that was how it went until Gavin returned, with apologies, as the twins were finishing their pudding, and Judith was suddenly reanimated and started talking again.

Sophy skipped the apricot sponge, and when she said, 'I think we should be saying goodnight,' Judith's expression said that it was high time, although she turned that into a smile. Judith said goodnight to Sophy too, and so did Gavin, so they weren't expecting her back. She was off to the nursery with the children, and that was her place, and the infatuation she had developed for Gavin would burn itself out pretty quickly if she had a scrap of pride in her.

She had a struggle getting the Romany princess undressed. Felicity wanted to sleep in her finery, and was at last dragged forcibly out of it and put into her cotton pyjamas. She sat up in bed glaring, telling Sophy, 'I hate you, I'm going to put a gipsy curse on you!'

'I think somebody did,' said Sophy. She was feeling wretched, her eyes were prickling, and Charles said sharply,

'Shut up, you're making her cry!'

Felicity's sulks vanished in a flash. 'I didn't mean it! You're not crying, are you?'

'Of course I'm not,' said Sophy.

She saw no more of Gavin or Judith that night. When she went down to the kitchen Mrs Greenhaugh had cleared the table, and Sophy stacked dishes in the dishwasher. Gavin and Judith were having coffee in the drawing room, and Sophy stayed in the little parlour off the kitchen for a while, then went back upstairs to her own room. She had persuaded Mrs Greenhaugh to stay in bed for an extra hour or so in the morning, and the drawing room door was shut and she didn't even glance towards it.

It was as well that Judith had turned up, or Sophy might have made a fool of herself. If she had, last Sunday night, Gavin would still have spent this week with Judith and tonight with Judith, and Sophy would have felt hurt and humiliated. Bitter too maybe, although she had no cause for bitterness. A man had made a pass at her and she had known it was because he felt sorry for her. It was comfort, not passion, he was offering, and it gave her no claims at all.

She got herself ready for bed and lay awake for hours because she was afraid to sleep. She knew now what the nightmare meant, when she ran down empty streets looking into empty houses. She had been a lonely child searching for love, and tonight again she was desolate and alone, and fear of sleepwalking, to Gavin's room again, which he was probably sharing with Judith, scared her to death.

She had put a chair on its side by her bed, so that if she did get up in the night she would fall over it, at the risk of waking the children as well as herself. Then she held off sleep until she could fight it no longer, and whatever she dreamed she did no walking.

She woke at the usual time and hurried downstairs, because she was in charge of breakfasts this morning, if Tom had held Mrs G. to her promise and stopped her getting up. Tom was in the kitchen, polishing a pair of black boots, and Gavin, in a suit that was very much the successful businessman, was sitting on the edge of the kitchen table, drinking black coffee.

Sophy hadn't expected to see Gavin so early. It was a little shock, and she had to swallow before she could answer his, 'Good morning.' He drained the coffee cup and put it down, then said, 'Right, I'm off.'

'But it's Sunday. You're not going in to work?' He worked all hours, but usually he seemed to be home on Sundays.

'That's where I'm going,' he said.

'Would Judith like a cup of tea or coffee?' She couldn't ask, 'In which room?'

'She'll come down when she does,' said Gavin, and Tom went on polishing his boots while Sophy went to lay the breakfast table. She got the children washed and dressed and fed, then sent them out into the garden where Tom was going to supervise the assembly of the kite. Then Mrs Greenhaugh came down, and grumbled at being made to sit quietly over a cup of tea and toast and marmalade.

But she did, while Sophy went into the drawing room to collect last night's coffee cups. The curtains were still closed and the room seemed full of shadows and Judith's perfume, and Sophy drew all the curtains back and opened a window. Then she began to put the coffee cups and the brandy glasses on the tray.

Judith had used pink lipstick yesterday, there was a smear of it on her cup, and Sophy was suddenly bone weary. I'm worn out already, she thought, and the day's hardly started. Of course she hadn't slept well and she wasn't looking forward to a day of Judith, who walked into the room at that moment, wearing the kimono with the poppies on it and a broad smile.

Had a good night? thought Sophy sourly. But of course you did. 'Good morning,' she said.

Judith flopped on to the chesterfield. 'Mrs G. has got you running around, hasn't she? The poor thing's past it, of course. God knows why Gavin keeps them on.'

Sophy almost smiled, because if Judith imagined that if she came here as mistress of this house she would persuade Gavin to put the Greenhaughs out to grass she hadn't a clue the kind of man he was. She asked, 'How about the twins? Maybe you'd like them to stay at school for the holidays too?' and Judith shrugged and went on smiling. 'Oh, I'm crazy about the children.'

It doesn't matter, Sophy thought, because Gavin would never let them be hurt. 'Look,' said Judith suddenly, 'I'm sorry about last night,' and Sophy almost dropped the tray. 'I shouldn't have snapped at you,' said Judith, 'but you have changed in the past month. Well, you know that, and we both know why, and it threw me at first.'

'We both know why?' Sophy echoed, and Judith leaned back, her silver hair shining against the wine red damask of the sofa.

'He only has to walk into a room and all the women's eyes light up. It's a sort of sexual electricity, it's not your fault you fancy him, they all do; but you're obviously the sensible sort, you're not going to be a pest, and I'm sorry I went for you.'

'Forget it,' said Sophy. This morning Judith seemed so sure of herself, and Gavin, that Sophy suspected that if she continued not being a pest she might even be allowed back here during the summer holidays. That would be fun. If she could bear to come.

'You've got a visitor,' said Mrs Greenhaugh, opening the drawing room door, and behind her stood Nick, looking his usual debonair self. Sophy gasped,

'What on earth brings you here?' She was proud of Nick and glad to see him. She said, 'This is my brother, Nicholas.' He had already introduced himself to Mrs Greenhaugh, but Judith said, 'Hello,' and she and Nick smiled at each other.

'Will you be staying for lunch?' asked Mrs Greenhaugh, and Nick said regretfully,

'I'd have liked that very much, but I do have to get back. Only I was over this way and I thought I'd look in on Sophy.' She wasn't as happy or as full of life as she had been last Sunday, but she was wearing the red jumper with her jeans and she stood tall, and he could see what the family meant about a change. 'I like to be sure my little sister's doing all right.' He grinned, and Judith laughed,

'Oh, she's doing better than all right. The children just adore her and she's been running the house singlehanded all week. Do make yourself at home. Have a drink. Do look after him, Sophy.'

Mrs Greenhaugh took the tray and Judith went too, and Sophy asked, 'Do you want a sherry?'

Nick was staring at the door that had just closed after Judith. 'Does he keep a harem? Yes, all right, I will have a drink.'

'Don't be daft! I'm the nanny. That's the girl-friend.' Sophy didn't say, 'The girl he's marrying,' although it probably was. She poured a dry sherry for him, and enquired, 'What brought you over this way?'

'You.' So he hadn't dropped in because he was here. This was a journey all for her.

'Why?' she asked, and Nick sat down and took a sip of the sherry and said, after rolling that round his palate, 'Because I missed you last Sunday and everybody who saw you seems to have been knocked sidewards, so I thought I'd come and see for myself.'

He took a long slow look. 'Growing up suits you,' he said. 'By the way, Cress sends her love.'

Sophy smiled wryly, 'Does she?'

'Cress has always been spoiled rotten,' said Nick. 'And she's always wanted to be the only pretty one. But she's fond of you. Take it from me she is.' He could be right. Sophy hoped he was. 'So am I,' he added, 'and some things about this set-up worry me.' Surely Nick wasn't going to warn her against Gavin too, not after meeting Judith. 'Such as, when did you really decide to leave home and go after a job?'

She considered for a moment, then said quietly, 'After I heard Peter telling you he wanted to finish with me.' She couldn't go into the full account. 'And this job was advertised, so I came and I got it.'

Nick bit his lip. 'You poor kid! I'm sorry.'

'Don't be.' Sophy put a reassuring hand on his shoulder, and smiled down when he looked up at her, 'Like you say,' she said, 'it's done me good, growing up. I *have* been running this house, and look around you. I was hardly trusted with the teacups at home, but I've broken nothing here. And my typing's improved like crazy. I've even been driving. In towns too, and I've enjoyed it.' She grinned. 'Pity about your wing, wasn't it, but I haven't scratched a thing since.'

'So long as you're not on the rebound,' he said, and her eyebrows shot up incredulously.

'From Peter, you mean? Falling for Gavin? Now you *have* seen Judith, so what do you think?'

'No chance,' said Nick, smiling too; and he stayed and chatted for another ten minutes, and when he got up to leave Sophy said,

'Give my love to everyone.'

'Including Cress?'

'Of course.'

'What about Pete?'

'What about Pete?' she mimicked, and the mischief in her face kept Nick smiling, although he thought seriously that somebody should be getting Pete Fisher and Sophy together again.

The kite lay on the lawn, a giant multi-coloured paper dragonfly, when Sophy went out into the garden looking for the twins. Tom had helped Charles put it together, and the little breeze that was blowing was enough to get the kite off the ground but not enough to fly it high. Charles had his eyes on the distant hills, but Sophy was preparing some of the lunch before she left the house and Charles was waiting for her fairly patiently.

When she did come out he ran to meet her, and then they discovered that Felicity was missing. Charles had ordered her away from his kite and she had flounced off in a huff, and they searched the gardens all around the house before Sophy spotted a flash of scarlet petticoat up among the green leaves and said, in a good clear voice, 'If she doesn't want to come with us we'll go on our own,' and then the gipsy princess came slithering down like a monkey.

An hour playing in the garden had taken the bandbox look from her costume, and Sophy said, 'I don't know about a princess, we're more the raggle-taggle gipsy-o this morning.'

Sophy loved the moors. She loved stepping through that old studded door in the wall into the land of gorse and heather. So did the children, and they liked it best of all when Gavin came with them. He had done, several times, and flying the kite today would have been more fun if he had been there.

'I wish Uncle Gavin had come,' sighed Felicity.

'He had to go to work,' Sophy explained.

'And she's here,' said Charles, 'and he'll go off with

her.' So he would, and where they went and what they did was no concern of Sophy's. She mustn't even think about it.

'It is getting windy, isn't it?' said Charles, and Felicity said kindly, 'When we get up the hill I shall make a big wind blow.'

She was convinced that she had. They climbed a high hill to the very top, and after a few abortive attempts the kite rose in the sky, dipping and soaring, and Felicity said, 'See, I told you,' and Sophy watched and thought how pretty it was. Concentrating on each moment as it came seemed the best way of getting through the day, and they flew the kite for the best part of an hour, with occasional squabbles as to who should hold the string but more or less amiably. Then they headed back home.

In the garden Judith was sitting on the bridge over the lake wearing her pale grey suede coat, and Sophy thought, she'll mess that up. And then, but I don't suppose she has to bother. She can always get it cleaned or buy another.

Judith was waiting for them. She didn't stand up when they reached her, but she said, 'I'm taking the Porsche to the works to meet Gavin. How did the kite make out?'

'Brilliant,' said Charles, and the children went on towards the house, but Judith gestured Sophy to hold back and Sophy had no choice. She didn't want to stay and listen because anything Judith had to say was unlikely to be good news, but she waited, and Judith said softly, 'Just one thing. I had a little chat with your brother after he left you and he mentioned this sleepwalking habit of yours.'

Sophy's cheeks began to burn. She had told her mother about the fuss of that first night. The family must have discussed it and perhaps Nick thought

Judith knew. It seemed she hadn't, but now her face
was sharp and suspicious. 'Oh, I believe you don't
know what you're doing when you're wandering
around in the dead of night in your night clothes. You
don't sleep starkers, I hope? Anyhow, I'm sure it's all
terribly innocent, and of course you are only here for
another week, but while you're here you wouldn't try
it on again, would you?'

Sophy had started to blush because she was
embarrassed, but now the angry blood rushed to her
head and she heard herself laugh and say into Judith's
astonished face, 'I don't know about that. That's the
thing about sleepwalking, you see, you just have no
idea where you're going to wake up.'

Judith started to laugh too, before Sophy had taken
more than a few strides, as though Sophy had been
joking. She fell into step beside her and said, 'I'll
listen out for you.' Then she said what a handsome
brother Sophy had and what did he do, and Sophy
said he was a lawyer and Judith said that was a handy
thing to have in the family.

But the Porsche went roaring down the drive and all
the time she had been talking Judith's eyes had been
glinting angrily, and Sophy knew she had made an
enemy. There was no way Judith would see Sophy as a
rival. But now she thought that Sophy might be a
nuisance, and she could be off to tell Gavin that.

I don't care, Sophy told herself. He knows I
wouldn't be. And I know, because it wouldn't be any
use if I was. She also told herself that she wouldn't be
sorry when the holidays ended. Surely nobody would
stop her keeping in touch with the children, and with
Mrs G. and Tom. But she started making plans for
herself from next week.

She would no longer be apprehensive about walking
around the shop or handling the antiques, and she

thought her mother and Cress might let her help
there. She would like that. She could learn from both
of them, especially her mother; and her social life was
going to be an improvement on the old round of baby-
sitting, going out with the girls and no real dates at all
before Peter.

In a way she would be going back to Peter, even if
he had taken up again with Anne Marie, and she
deliberately set about trying to recapture some of her
old feelings for him.

It was only a month since she had thought he was
wonderful, and she listened to one of his favourite
songs, Neil Diamond singing *Summer Love*, on her
cassette player in the study while the twins watched a
TV children's programme in the drawing room.

The memories came back as she sat in an armchair
letting the words and music brainwash her, and she
soon had Peter's image vividly in her mind. It would
have been an odd thing if she couldn't recall him after
only four weeks, and there was no pain now. But not
a lot of joy either. No rising excitement, not even
when she imagined him coming closer and closer.
Nothing like hunger for him, let alone starvation. But
perhaps it would come. Or something would.

The phone rang and she went to answer it, with
Neil Diamond still singing in the background, and
when Peter spoke she blurted, 'Good heavens, I was
just thinking about you.'

'Were you?' he sounded gratified. Then he sobered.
'I've been talking to Nick.' Nick had done a lot of
talking today. 'He told me you heard us that Sunday.'

'Yes.'

'Any chance of seeing you tonight?' She had been
trying to 'see' Peter, and this was the real thing. He
would get her out of the house and out of herself, and
she had felt down since Judith arrived. She had always

suspected that Judith might sap her self-confidence, but a few hours with Peter could boost it. She could glamorise herself and see what effect that had, but she hesitated, and he said eagerly, I could be over in half an hour. We could go out for a meal. I really do want to talk to you, just name the time and place.'

He had never shown any particular impatience before. Sophy had always been the amenable one, but now Peter was anxious to oblige, and when she said, 'You know where I am?' he said, 'Nick told me the way, I'll be right over.'

'At Gavin Tighe's,' she said. 'And make it an hour.'

When she put down the phone she turned to see Felicity standing in the doorway of the drawing room. 'Was that the one you wanted?' Felicity asked.

'What?'

'The phone call.'

'Oh,' Sophy smiled. 'Yes, I suppose it was,' and Felicity looked as smug as she had on the hilltop when the kite went up. Bless her, thought Sophy, she thinks she's fixed it for me. 'Let's see if Mrs G. can cope with you two,' she said.

Mrs G. could, of course. She thought it was time that Sophy took a night off and insisted on handing over a key, although Sophy assured her that she would be back at a reasonable hour.

Peter is coming for me, Sophy told her reflection in the bedroom mirror, and smiled at herself and was sure she was feeling happier by the minute. She put blusher on her cheeks and a dusting of eyeshadow with golden glints so that her eyes sparkled and her face glowed. She wore the coral silk pants again, with the matching shirt and the bronze sandals; and was downstairs waiting when the heavy knocker on the front door was banged a couple of times and she opened the door to Peter.

Oh, he was the same, just the same. She was so pleased to see him that she hugged him like a long-lost friend, smiling broadly. Peter had been told how well Sophy was looking by so many people that he was prepared for something surprising. Nicholas had said this afternoon, 'She heard us talking that Sunday morning and she just ran away, but she's got herself together since and she did ask to be remembered to you.'

Others had told him of seeing her in the park, with Gavin Tighe—'You know, Tighe Industries,' and the whole thing had been a shaker. So was Sophy, standing back from him now, suggesting with wry mockery, 'Would you like a conducted tour of the Tighe House, as you admire him so much?' Peter grinned and shook his head.

'Right with you, then,' she said, and picked up her purse from a table, and a brown mohair jacket from a chair, and went out with him to his car that was parked in front of the house. He shook his head again. Her clothes made a world of difference, her hair was different, her make-up. But the real change was under the skin and as he started up the car he asked, 'How did you get this job?'

'Sheer luck,' she said. 'My number must have come up that day.'

He began to say he was sorry she had overheard his talk with Nick, and she thought he might have gone on to explain that she had been jumping to conclusions, he hadn't meant them to finish, if she hadn't interrupted with, 'You were right, I must have been a drag. I hear you're dating Anne Marie again.'

'Once,' he said.

He turned right at the end of the drive, towards the village, and she saw the lights of a car in the distance on the left, and twisted in her seat to watch it turn into the drive. She was sure it was the Merc. That meant that the Porsche had been left at the works because Judith would have come back with Gavin. 'I said "Who told you that?",' said Peter, obviously repeating himself, and Sophy said, 'Cress, but she's a romantic. She thinks that Gavin is my lover as well as my boss.'

She didn't know why she said that, except that the thought of Gavin and Judith together tied her in knots and saying something fairly outrageous released the tension.

'And is he?' asked Peter.

She might say, 'No, but he would have been if I'd had a second chance.' She might always have this crazy dream that if she had taken the first chance Judith would not have come. But these were things she could never tell anyone. 'Would it surprise you?' she asked, and Peter took his eyes from the road for a quick glance at the girl beside him and said, 'It would have poleaxed me. But now—I don't know.'

'And why should you?' She would deny it some time, she supposed, but for now Peter could believe what he liked. He was shaken, but he was intrigued, and he was becoming more fascinated all the time. He had been very fond of Sophy. He had thought she was sweet but dim, and as she laughed and talked now he couldn't believe that that quick mind had been locked inside her head. He could see how she might attract even a man as eligible as Tighe. Her smooth young skin seemed to exude a potently sexy perfume.

All their earlier dates had been tepid affairs, with Sophy listening and saying nothing much, wearing something enveloping. But tonight the silk shirt fitted smoothly over her high firm breasts, and Peter couldn't think why he had ever imagined her eyes were grey. They looked golden-green in the candle-light.

As they'd coasted around, looking for somewhere to eat, they had passed the pub where she had had a meal with Gavin when she drove the Mini for the first time, and she had told Peter that story, and had him laughing and protesting, 'You're putting me on. He never nearly got into a punch-up over your driving.'

'No,' she said, 'he just looked at the man and scared him silly.' They were turning into the car park, and she said quickly, 'Not here. We'll have a Chinese meal. You like Chinese food, don't you? There's a restaurant in Buxham.'

She drank quite a lot during the meal, flirting, enjoying herself, and when Peter said, 'Even your eyes seem to have changed colour, it's like seeing a kitten turn into a tiger—why didn't all this happen for me?' she said gaily,

'Perhaps it takes one to know one,' and thought how glib and trite that sounded. And she smiled into Peter's eyes, because not long ago she had wanted him to make love to her more than anything, and if he did it might be good and it might be enough. She smiled and touched the back of his hand, her trailing fingertips sensuous and promising.

She knew what she was promising. In the car she sat with her head on his shoulder, and when he drew up in a lay-by on a lonely road about a mile away from the house, she slipped into his arms. 'You're beautiful,' he mumbled against her hair, and Sophy thought, not really but nearly.

He kissed her face and her lips, and she wound her arms tightly around his neck, but when he began to caress her breasts she shuddered. She wasn't relaxing, she was tensing up, and this had to be the wrong place and time, but she only had herself to blame when her belated reluctance sparked off a slight struggle.

Peter did let her go, after a moment or two, and she

gasped breathless excuses. 'I'm sorry, only it is late. Nearly midnight,' nodding towards the dashboard clock, 'and I promised to be in by eleven. I'll be home from next weekend. Would you like to come round on Monday evening, a week today?'

That mollified him, and he drove her back and kissed her tenderly on the mouth and said he would ring her tomorrow. 'Yes,' she said, 'thank you,' as the car drove away.

There was a light on in the hall, but she used the key to let herself in, and was hurrying towards the stairs when Gavin opened the study door. Her lipstick was probably smudged all over her face and her hair must look like a bird's nest. She hadn't wanted to be seen by anybody, least of all by him. He looked impassively at her. 'Pleasant evening?'

'Yes, thank you,' she said, for the second time in two minutes.

'It didn't end in rape?'

'*What?* Of *course* not!' She wasn't that dishevelled, but then she glanced down and froze, because her shirt was gaping open to the waist.

'Just a rather enthusiastic close encounter?' Gavin sounded cynically amused. 'You'd better fasten a few buttons in case Mr G. or Tom are still around.'

Her tongue was cleaving to the roof of her mouth, and he had closed the door before she could say anything. If she could have thought of anything to say.

CHAPTER EIGHT

'DID you have a super time?' was almost the first thing Felicity said next morning, and Sophy, who felt terrible, said, 'Absolutely lovely.'

Felicity beamed and looked for her gipsy costume, and Sophy picked it up from the chair over which it was draped and said, 'We'd better get this washed if you want to wear it tomorrow when Lester and Joe and Harvey come. And mended,' poking her finger through a tear in the skirt. 'It's jeans for you today, princess.'

She took the dress down to the kitchen, to handwash it. Today was wash-day, Agnes would be along to help Mrs Greenhaugh, but although the label inside declared the small garment washable the brilliant colours could run into the rest of the wash, and that wouldn't please Mrs G.

The breakfast room door was open, Gavin's cup and plate had been used, but there was no sign of him, and Sophy was glad, because after last night she was in no hurry to face him again. She hadn't seen Judith, but that didn't mean Judith wasn't in the house, just that she wasn't an early riser.

'Have a nice time with your young man?' Mrs Greenhaugh greeted Sophy, and she said,

'Yes, thank you,' checking the impulse to stress that Peter was not her anything. 'May I swill this through?'

She went to the empty sink and whisked soap flakes into warm water and proceeded to dunk the dress, enquiring, 'Is Judith still with us?'

'No,' said Mrs G., 'but I expect she'll be back soon.'

She came and went at her own sweet whim, it seemed. 'Mr Gavin left early,' Mrs G. added. 'Something seems to be on at the works.' There was a note in her voice that made Sophy look up and ask,

'Everything all right?'

'Bound to be,' said Mrs G. 'Always is. I never did understand any of it.' But her smile seemed strained and thoughts flashed through Sophy's mind: Suppose Tighe Industries is into a bad patch. Firms do crash these days, big names, without even a hint getting around beforehand. Suppose he came back tonight and said he was broke.

That would be awful, tragic, but in a small and selfish way it would have a silver lining, making Gavin less eligible and less out of reach.

'You're very quiet,' remarked Mrs G., and Sophy was holding the dress over the sink, water streaming from it, frozen in an impossible dream. She jumped, and dropped the dress into a bowl, collecting pegs and making for the door that led outside while Mrs G. mused, 'That's how the house is going to be most of the time from next week, with you and the children gone. You've been a good girl, I'll be sorry to lose you.'

'I'll miss you too,' said Sophy. She pegged the dress out in the little courtyard and it fluttered like a bright flag, and the thought of next week was drab as though there was nothing ahead of her but grey days.

She took the children out for the day, driving into the Lake District, sailing on a launch on Lake Windermere, and all the while she was conscious how time was passing. She had always known that the job was temporary. Perhaps it was seeing Peter again, so much a part of her other life, but from this morning there was something inexorable in the way hour after hour slipped by, like the heavy ticking of a clock inside her.

This was her last Monday, soon it would be her last day. The bedtime story was lasting the course, she hadn't realised what a fund of invention she had. With the twins in bed she stitched the rip in Felicity's skirt and spun tonight's tale, and then laid out the gipsy finery for tomorrow morning and leaned over to kiss goodnight.

Felicity's arms went round her neck. 'You're happy now, aren't you?' said Felicity. 'You don't have to listen for phone calls any more.'

Sophy had stopped listening a while ago. Peter had said he would ring today and he probably would, but if the phone rang she wouldn't hold her breath as she had in those early days. She said, 'I should just think I am happy,' and she put on a happy face, with the grin of a Cheshire cat, that had them both giggling.

She came out of their bedroom before the grin had faded and Gavin was sitting in the armchair. She hadn't heard him, and the sight of him wiped the smile from her face. 'Don't stop smiling for me,' he said, 'I'm glad somebody's happy.' He went in to say goodnight to the children, he had been waiting for her to finish the story, and she wondered, what shall I say when he comes out?

They were telling him what they had been doing all day, with the usual hair-raising embellishments. She might talk about the day too, or she might say, 'Sorry about last night. Wasn't it lucky Mrs G. wasn't in the hall? Would you believe my shirt just came undone? No, you wouldn't, not five buttons. Would you believe that Peter isn't the love of my life, not my love at all? You might believe me, but you wouldn't care.'

As he came back she asked, 'Any typing?'

He said, 'Yes, there is some you could do,' and

Sophy followed him downstairs into the study. There
were papers on the desk. Most of the time there were
papers on the desk in here, and phone calls to the
house, and always there were the factories, and other
offices that were the real heart of his empire. Mrs
Greenhaugh didn't understand the ramifications of the
business, but she sensed that Gavin was worried and
nobody knew him better than she did, and Sophy
heard herself say, 'Mrs G. thought there might be
trouble at mill.'

'What?' Gavin looked up, frowning, the words
had been flippant and nosy and she said, 'Oh,
nothing.'

He didn't press it. He pushed over several sheets of
figures and said, 'Type those out for me, would you?'
Then he sat down and took another sheaf of papers out
of a briefcase and went into a brown study over them.

Typing figures that meant nothing to you wasn't so
simple. She had to concentrate and keep her thoughts
from straying. She thought, I'll go temping as a
secretary. I'll emigrate. And then—I must be crazy, I
could meet him again as easily on the other side of the
world.

She hit a wrong letter and stared down at it, as
though it might dissolve and obviate the need for
erasing, and the phone rang. Gavin picked it up, said,
'Hello,' and to Sophy, 'Your mother.'

'Shall I take it——?' She looked towards the door,
and the extension in the hall, and he said,

'That's all right,' and turned back to his papers.

Her mother began telling her how she had just had
to ring, to say how pleased she was that Sophy and
Peter were still seeing each other. 'We've all been a
little bit worried about you. Even Nick.' Nick's name
came with a light laugh, because it was unusual for
Nick to worry about anybody. 'Were you surprised

when he walked in yesterday morning?' her mother asked, and Sophy said wryly,

'Yesterday was a surprising day altogether.'

'He told us about meeting Judith. He had quite a chat with her. He said she seems a very nice girl and very fond of you.'

She couldn't stand here, nattering about Judith, and she muttered, 'Oh, there's a real rapport going there. Look, I'll be home at the weekend, but I am rather busy now.'

She had hardly reseated herself when the phone rang again. Again Gavin answered and again he held it out, this time wordlessly, to her. This time it was Peter, who said, 'I can't tell you how good it was to see you yesterday. I'm counting the hours till next Monday.' He had a couple of dates lined up. They had been asked to a party by one of his colleagues, so he must have been putting it around that he and Sophy were a twosome. And there was a film showing locally next week, that she might like to see. She said something about that being a good idea, uncomfortably conscious of Gavin's fingers drumming the top of the desk.

'I have to hang up now,' she said.

'I'll ring tomorrow,' said Peter, and automatically she murmured,

'That would be lovely. Sorry,' she said to Gavin, 'they both came at once.'

'You're not expecting any more?'

'No.'

'Good, because I am.'

From then on she typed in silence until Gavin's call came. His voice was brusque and she thought, It isn't going well, whatever it is. He looked across at her and said, 'There's no hurry for that. Can you finish it tomorrow?' He meant, Get out, and Sophy said, 'Of course,' and closed the door behind her.

A long time later as she sat at her window she saw him walk out into the garden below. He went from the lights of the house into the shadows of the moonlight, a tall solitary figure. Perhaps he was just strolling round the garden, or perhaps he would walk the moors half the night, Mrs G. said he sometimes did that when he had problems on his mind, and instinctively she jumped to her feet to follow him.

But before she reached the door of her room she stopped. Gavin walked alone because he wanted to be alone. He wasn't going to share business confidences with Sophy. He didn't need her sympathy and certainly not her advice. Her reaction was to run after him into the darkness, but she had to get it into her head that there was nothing at all that Gavin Tighe needed or wanted from her.

Next morning he was leaving the house as she came downstairs with the children, and although he stopped to say goodbye to them his mind was on other things. 'He's like a bear with a sore head these days,' said Mrs G., sounding quite worried. But the children were full of the Robinsons, due here this morning; they gave Sophy no time to brood. They would have gobbled their breakfasts at a rate guaranteed to give anyone indigestion if she hadn't kept telling them that Joe and Lester and Harvey were unlikely to turn up before ten o-clock.

The Robinson's Volvo came up the drive at ten minutes to ten, with Mary at the wheel, and as soon as it stopped the three boys erupted from the back. Felicity, in her gipsy finery, took them aback for a moment, but they all thought she looked super, and Sophy and Mary followed the stampede into the house and up to the nursery toy cupboard.

'Thank heavens this is the last week of the holidays,'

said Mary fervently. 'Do your two go back on Monday?'

'Sunday,' said Sophy.

'It's a lovely house.' Mary had been looking around as they climbed the staircase, 'And they're grand kids. Shall you be coming here to look after them again?'

Not if Judith had any say in it. Sophy said, 'I don't know,' and met Mary's kind and knowing eyes and thought, She guesses I've fallen for Gavin. Nobody would believe me if I denied it. But so long as nobody suspects how badly they won't feel too sorry for me. She laughed and said, 'No harm in hoping, though, because I've had a super time, but all good things come to an end.'

It was an energetic day. After a comparatively quiet half hour in the nursery the twins took the Robinsons out to see their 'tree house', and they climbed trees and raced around the gardens, playing tag and hide-and-seek and, 'Watch me, I'm Tarzan!' They had lunch on the lawn by the lake, and Mrs Greenhaugh packed a picnic tea for them to take over the moors in the afternoon, and they flew the kite.

When the visitors clambered back into their car the children were half asleep, and their mother wound down the window to say goodbye to Sophy, 'It's been a lovely day, it really has. Come and see us as soon as you get home, won't you?' She paused and asked, 'How long is it you've been here?'

'Getting on for five weeks,' said Sophy, and Mary laughed,

'Well, nobody would believe it.' She meant the change in Sophy, but Sophy thought, I can't believe it's ending; and she knew that she had better believe it, because it was.

When the twins were safely in bed she went down to the study to finish the typing for Gavin. He wasn't home yet, and at about the same time as last night she got a phone call from Peter. She could remember when Peter's voice had made her heart leap, but now it didn't do a thing. She sat on the edge of Gavin's desk and began to doodle flowers on a piece of paper, listening to Peter telling her how much better it would be next week when they were together again. He was taking it for granted that they would be together. He had Nick's blessing and her parents' blessing; and now he wouldn't be ashamed to be seen anywhere with her, thanks to the sophistication she had acquired, living with Gavin Tighe.

'Gavin Tighe,' she wrote, on the page of doodles of daisies, and smiled down at it because she liked the look of the name. 'I love you,' she scrawled underneath. 'I've got some work to do,' she said, 'I must ring off.'

After she had put down the phone she sat looking at the paper, and then she read, softly, 'Gavin Tighe, I love you,' and knew that she had gone beyond gratitude or infatuation. There was lust in it. She yearned for him, ached for him, but love was so much more; and she was so deep in love that it would probably last the rest of her life. Wherever she went and whatever she did she would always hope that he was going to walk through the door.

She tore up the pieces of paper into very small pieces and dropped it like confetti into the waste basket. There wasn't a chance. Judith would see to that. Gavin liked Sophy well enough, but he would say goodbye to her at the end of the week and probably never give her another thought. Until the next school holidays when, unless Judith had the final word, she might be asked to come back.

Even when she had finished the typing she was reluctant to leave the study. After his bedroom this was the room in the house that was private and personal to him. She had spent several evenings in here and, until last night, she had felt relaxed and easy working with him, learning a little of the scope of his business enterprises.

There was a filing cabinet, drawers in the desk. Mrs Greenhaugh thought something was going wrong, and there could be clues all around if Sophy understood the language and had the nerve to go through the papers. She wished she knew. It seemed a long time ago that she had stood in that boardroom and asked him, 'Where do you go from here?'

'Straight ahead,' he'd told her, and she'd said, 'I wish you well.' He had such confidence and such power. His grandfather, who ran a nice little business, was easily satisfied, but Gavin was never satisfied, and a man like that could overreach. Of course Sophy wished him well, with all her heart. But if his empire was starting to crumble, she thought with wry humour, please tell Judith and then she might go away, and I might find the courage to walk at night again. Awake this time. And please tell her soon, because I only have a few nights left.

That was crazy thinking. He would weather any storm, and even if a storm was coming he wouldn't be clinging to Sophy. She couldn't imagine him clinging to anyone, certainly not to Judith.

She stayed where she was, and passed the time rattling off some of the stories she had made up for the twins. She would leave them behind her when she left, and if she didn't come back it would be something to remember her by. When the door opened it was after ten o'clock, but it still wasn't Gavin. 'How much longer are you going to be at this?' demanded Mrs Greenhaugh, and Sophy smiled,

'This isn't work, I'm writing a story for the twins.'

'Come and have your supper, then,' she was ordered.

'Is Gavin home?' She hadn't heard the car but she had been typing, but Mrs Greenhaugh said, 'He rang during the afternoon to say he was working and wouldn't be back tonight.'

There was no reason why Sophy should have been told. She had gone straight into the study from the nursery, but it was hard to hide her disappointment and keep smiling and say lightly, 'Judith, I expect.'

'I don't think so,' said Mrs Greenhaugh, looking glum.

It rained next day, a thin grey drizzle, persistent and depressing. Sophy and Mrs Greenhaugh were sewing name tabs on new clothes that the children would be taking back to school for the summer term, and this brought home to the twins that the holiday was coming to an end. They were a little subdued, settling down uncharacteristically to a quiet game in the drawing room, while Mrs G. and Sophy sat and stitched.

Sophy had been the best nanny they had ever had, they told her, and looking at them now she had the sensation that time was not just running out but rushing by. Every minute was precious. She must hold the memories of this room and the children. And of Gavin. She kept her head bowed over her sewing, but her eyes blurred with tears so that she could hardly see, and she thought how awful it would be if she did break down when she had to go away, knowing she might never see him again.

If it killed her she had to go smiling, and she blinked hard and bit off the piece of cotton as she finished a name tag. 'You'll cut through the enamel of your teeth doing that,' said Mrs Greenhaugh severely. 'Use the scissors.'

'Look what I've found!' said Charles.

The children were playing marbles on a smooth patch of carpet, and he had gone round the back of a chair to retrieve one that had rolled out of bounds. He had half the head of the little Staffordshire pottery Turk in his hand, and Mrs Greenhaugh gave an anguished yelp, looking up at the shelf where the Turk should have been sitting, then going over, looking all over the floor, demanding, 'Where's the rest of him?'

There was no rest. Half a head was all there was. Whoever had broken the little ornament had almost cleared away the pieces, and Sophy said, 'I dusted in here on Saturday, he wasn't broken then.'

She frowned queryingly at the twins, but their denials rang true, and if they had smashed anything they would have said so, they wouldn't have hidden it. She couldn't think who would. Unless Gavin had cleared it away, if it was beyond repair, and not thought to mention it. There had been no accidents yesterday while the Robinsons were here.

Mrs Greenhaugh took a personal pride in all these things. Sophy was the only one she had trusted to care for them, and she held the brightly painted shard, with its one askew eye, in the palm of her hand, and her face puckered. Then she looked up at Sophy and Sophy said, 'I didn't do it.'

'I'm sure you didn't,' said Mrs Greenhaugh, but Sophy felt she was not quite sure, that she could be regretting letting Sophy handle her treasures, and remembered the bottle Sophy had dropped in the bathroom on her first morning here. 'It might have been mended,' said Mrs Greenhaugh, 'if whoever did it had spoken up.'

'Maybe it was Gavin,' said Sophy.

'Maybe it was,' said Mrs Greenhaugh, but that put another constraint on the day. After that Mrs

Greenhaugh seemed as depressed as Sophy, and when Gavin came home that evening he said he had no idea how the little Turk had been broken. Nor did he seem to care much.

Nobody mentioned it again. Sophy did wonder about the twins, it was possible, and she wondered—if she hadn't been leaving this weekend—if Mrs Greenhaugh would have decided she no longer needed Sophy's help with anything valuable and fragile.

Peter was ringing regularly. As soon as she saw him Sophy would have to set the record straight. She had outgrown him, she was no longer the dreaming girl. But she couldn't make that kind of statement on the phone in somebody else's house. She could only be friendly and casual when he rang her, and as brief as possible, and after the way she had carried on on Sunday night Peter was due for an apology too.

He offered to drive over and collect her, 'Any time over the weekend,' and she thanked him, with excuses.

'But I probably won't be home till Monday. The children go back to school Sunday afternoon, I may go along with them.'

She would like to, if she was asked; and there was a chance that Gavin would give her a lift home if she had no transport, and that would be half an hour together in which they might talk.

There wasn't much talking with Gavin the last two days. Sophy didn't see much of him either, he came late and went early, and then it was Saturday night and the twins were sitting up in bed, listening to the last bedtime story. She made it a long one. She had brought the children on the magic island, whose names were of course Charles and Felicity, to the spiky little jungle where the tyger lived, and she had intended finishing it tonight. Bringing them face to face with the tyger, and a happy ending, of course. But she couldn't make it final. She said, 'That's all for now,' and tucked them up and kissed them goodnight.

If she came back she would go on with it. If not— well, it was only a story, they had books full of stories. The children would miss her, but by the time the next holidays came round she would only be a memory. And Mrs Greenhaugh suspected her of dropping the little Turk, and Gavin had no place for her. So her chances of returning were remote.

She would go on with her own life, but oh, how she wished now that she had stayed in Gavin's arms that night, and tonight she wished she had the nerve to go 'sleepwalking'. He was home. He had arrived when everyone was in bed. She had heard his car in the still night and gone to her window and seen the light come on in the study below. It was after midnight, he might not be alone, but she could go down and ask if he wanted coffee, or anything. Only the light went out almost at once and Sophy went slowly back to bed.

She told herself that, if she could have been sure he was alone, she would have gone to find him. To thank him for the past five weeks. She might have explained about Peter and asked if Gavin was worried about work, and was there any way she could make things easier for a little while.

Lying here, in the darkness, she could imagine herself saying all that, but she knew that if the lights were turned on and she was face to face with him, even if he was quite alone, the words wouldn't come. She buried her face in the pillow and prayed, if I sleepwalk tonight let me go the same way and wake with Gavin beside me again.

But she woke next morning, still in bed, to the sound of sobbing—shrill childish wails that had Sophy racing into the children's room, where Felicity was sitting, bolt upright, the picture of woe, with tears pouring down her cheeks. As Sophy sat on the bed and hugged her Charles said cheerfully, 'She always does it. She'll be right as rain as soon as we get there.'

'But it's been so lovely this time with you here.' Felicity pressed her damp little face into Sophy's shoulder, 'and I won't be able to wear my princess dress again for ages!'

They both looked solemn and sweet, in grey school uniform and small scarlet blazers, getting into the car to go back to school. Gavin was taking them, but nobody had suggested that Sophy went too. She was kissed goodbye with Mrs Greenhaugh and Tom, and stood with them in a little group.

'You'll come back for the next holidays, won't you, Sophy?' Charles asked from the back seat of the car, leaning round Felicity, who said sadly,

'I expect Sophy's getting married and he might not let her come.'

'For goodness' sake——' Sophy began to protest.

'Girls do.' Felicity was regretting having wished that Sophy's friend would turn up, even if it had made Sophy happy. She would have liked all the holidays to be like this one, she didn't want anything to change. 'But you wouldn't, would you?' she said to Gavin, who laughed and said,

'I might, one of these days.' The car door was closed and the car drew away, and Sophy waved and smiled, and beside her Tom sighed and said, 'They're young rips, but every time you miss 'em.'

'*Are* you getting married?' asked Mrs Greenhaugh.

'Of course I'm not!' Never. She would never marry, and the thought of Gavin marrying filled her with an almost insane jealousy, as though she would go mad if she dwelt on it.

'Then why don't you stay on?' said Mrs

Greenhaugh, and Sophy, who had been walking slowly back to the house, stopped dead.

'*Here?*'

'Where else would I be talking about? You've been a big help. I'd like you to stay.'

She could help Mrs G., type for Gavin, see him, talk to him. But one of these days he might marry Judith, and when Judith heard of this offer she might well dig in her heels and get Sophy out.

'What about Judith?' said Sophy. 'She doesn't like me much.'

They went into the house, walking down the hall and passing the drawing room, and Mrs Greenhaugh nodded grimly at the drawing room door and said,

'I know, and I've got more than a sneaking suspicion that she did that. She phoned on Thursday and I asked her about it and she said it had got to be you, as you were the one who handled them, and wasn't it a good job you'd only got a few more days to go.'

That proved nothing, except Judith's dislike of Sophy. But Judith could have smashed the little ornament, and left one telltale fragment, and it could have turned Mrs Greenhaugh against Sophy.

'If Judith feels that strongly about getting me out what does Gavin feel about it?' Sophy asked quietly.

'He isn't married to her yet.' Mrs Greenhaugh began to fill the kettle. 'And he thinks it's a very good idea, he hopes I'll persuade you. So now shall we have a cup of tea and talk about it? You haven't got anything else lined up, have you?'

'I haven't got another job.' Sophy wanted to say yes, and pin her hopes on what Mrs Greenhaugh had said, he isn't married yet. But that would be prolonging the agony of parting. Gavin thought it would be fine if she stayed. Mrs Greenhaugh needed help, the children needed supervision during the holidays, and Sophy was willing and able, and got on with everybody except Judith. But she loved him, and she didn't know if she was strong enough to stay under his roof, hiding it all the time. She did know that if Judith became his wife she wouldn't be able to endure another night here.

She asked, 'Can I think about it?'

Mrs Greenhaugh said of course, and Sophy spent most of the rest of the day out of the house. She went over the moors, like Gavin did, and if he wasn't here in person he filled her thoughts to the exclusion of everything else. But she still couldn't give an answer when she said goodnight to Mrs G. and Tom. She said she thought she should discuss it with her parents first, just ask them how they felt about her staying here more or less permanently. Mrs Greenhaugh agreed that was reasonable, but Sophy knew that her mother would say, 'Come home.' So would Nick and Cress. And Peter. She wouldn't ask any of them for advice, she was stalling for time; and she sat in the empty nursery, knowing that the problem was hers alone. Tomorrow she must make the decision, and whichever way she took there was going to be pain.

She almost wished she hadn't been given the chance to stay. She sat, hands clenched, trying to be calm, to consider this offer as a job. She paced the room, trying to hold down the turmoil of emotions that swept away everything except a longing to be where Gavin was.

She was pacing when the door opened and he stood there, and her breath caught. 'Burning the midnight oil?' he asked. He must have seen the light round the door. She didn't know he was home, and she said jerkily,

'I have a problem.'

'Haven't we all?' He walked across to the map on the wall. Another little character had been drawn on at each day during the holidays, but there would be no more. He had his back to Sophy and she asked, 'Business?'

'All the time. And a few more problems than usual in the last few days.'

'I'm sorry.' She wished he would tell her about it. His shoulders were broad, but she longed to put a hand on them and offer some small support. But when he turned he smiled, 'Nothing that doesn't get resolved. Them I can handle. Now, what's your problem?'

So work wasn't worrying him, and she knew with a flash of intuition that he thrived on the challenges of big business. There he was a winner who would go on winning. She said, 'Mrs G.'s asked me to stay on and help her run the house.'

'And?'

'If you're marrying Judith I don't think she'd want me around.'

'And if I'm not?'

It was like constricting bands around her chest snapping. She took a deep deep breath. He must have been teasing the twins. But Judith would still be here, it would still be hell at times. 'I just don't know,' she said.

'Whether you want to run back home?' Gavin was getting impatient with her and she couldn't blame him. She must seem a ditherer, and he was looking at her as though somebody should shake some sense into her.

'Well, this is a very small problem, I know,' she said shrilly. 'But there are things to be said for and against. I've been weighing them up all day, trying to make up my mind.' She started walking up and down again, using her hands to emphasise her points, right hand, left hand. 'Like, I enjoy being here very much. I'm very fond of Mrs G., and Tom, and I love the house, I'd enjoy helping to run it. But, if I go home, I think my mother would let me help in the antique shop and I think I'd enjoy that too.'

She wanted him to say, 'Stay here, we need you.' That could be enough to tip the balance. When she paused he said,

'It wouldn't be a simple housekeeping job. There's secretarial work you could do, and your salary would be adjusted, of course.'

But it was all pure business, and she knew that if she did stay she would make a fool of herself one day or night. She felt an overwhelming physical pull towards him that made her head swim, and she gripped the table's edge, holding herself steady.

'All right, let's have the facts.' He had lost patience. He glared at her so that she almost cowered. 'Your real reason for going back would be Fisher. I thought you'd have more sense than to go after somebody weak enough to be influenced by a load of claptrap in a magazine. If he was. And if he wasn't he's a bloody bad judge of character. He doesn't know the first thing about you and he never will. What are you? A masochist? Can't you see how stupid you'd be, taking up with him again?'

It was true. Anyway, she wouldn't. But Gavin's contempt sparked anger in her, and she gave a derisive hoot. '*I'm* stupid? Ha! Well now, I've never said anything about Judith, but if you're such a marvellous judge of character yourself how come you can't see she's poison? I'm sure she's terrific in bed, but I'm glad to hear you're not marrying her, because oh, boy would she cause havoc in the household!'

'Yes,' he said.

'You know?'

'I've always known.'

'Oh!' It was very quiet. It was late. The house, the village, was asleep. But their voices had been raised, filling the room, and now it seemed you could have heard a pin drop. Then Sophy asked, 'You want me to stay?' and Gavin looked straight at her,

'I'll keep you here by force if I have to.'

'You're joking!' He wasn't smiling, and he didn't smile. He said,

'I don't think I am, but I'd rather we didn't put it to the test. Please *stay*.' The word came out with emphasis, sharp and staccato, then he went on in level tones, as though he was making a report. 'I'll tell you why I want you to stay. You remember when we went to the works, almost as soon as you came here?' She nodded. She found she was hanging on to the table again. 'And you asked me where I was going, and I said "Straight ahead". When I said that, for the first time, I felt it might be better not to go alone. That it might be good to have somebody like you with me. The typing I brought home wasn't that urgent, it could have been done by the office staff, but I wanted you in the room with me. When I was away that week I wanted to come back to you.'

She whispered, 'Judith came too.'

'Judith came to Cannock on the Friday, I hadn't asked her to come and I saw very little of her except for driving her back. There've been a number of Judiths in my life, but there'll be no more.' He was still speaking in level tones that betrayed no emotion, but his dark eyes were unfathomable. 'I hadn't thought about you leaving, going away. I'd thought about us being together—I'd thought a lot about that—and I thought I had time to let you forget the man you'd told me you loved.

'And then, on Sunday night, he turned up, and that was when I realised how completely I was committed.

It wouldn't be somebody like you. It would be you or nobody. I went through the tortures of the damned waiting for you to come back, and when you did I could have pulled the house down around our ears. Believe me, It's an understatement to say I've had a hellish week.'

He paused briefly, then went on, 'And that's how it is. I hoped Mrs G. would persuade you to stay, and that time would be on my side. It seems she hasn't, so now I'm asking you, because if I don't marry you I'll never marry anyone.' His voice was changing now, becoming harsher, sounding desperate, 'You don't love him. Perhaps you did as a child, but not as a woman, because you're my woman. So, for God's sake, Sophy, stay and let me try to teach you to love me.'

She should have stopped him before. She should have rushed at him, crying, 'I love you,' but it was wonderful and incredible, this proud and marvellous man telling her how he needed her. She knew that he had never pleaded before, and she flew to him now. 'Sunday night,' she said, 'it wasn't so much a close encounter as a small scuffle. And it wasn't just the wrong time and place, it was the wrong man.'

That hit him the same time as she did. He put his arms around her and started to smile. 'I'll kill him!'

'Please don't. Some of it was my fault. I'm going to say sorry next time I see him, but I don't want to see him again.'

'Give him my regards,' said Gavin, 'and offer him a job if he wants one.'

That would be quite a prize for Peter. 'That should console him,' she said, 'Please kiss me.' He kissed her gently, holding her so tight that she felt as if they were growing together. Sophy pressed herself against him, moulding her body to his, and he said,

'Do you know what you're doing?'

She could hear the thudding of his heart and feel its echo in her blood, and they were close, but she wanted him closer, he could never be too close. 'Oh yes,' she said, 'I know.'

'The last time I thought I'd been rushing things.' He began to trace the contours of her face with a finger, and when he touched her lips her small white teeth trapped his fingertip, biting gently.

'The last time,' she said, 'Cress warned me against letting you make love to me because I might get addicted.'

'I hope so,' he said. 'I think I might guarantee it.'

'I wouldn't mind being rushed.'

The next kiss was long and loving, and he swung her up into his arms and carried her, kissing her, and when he laid her down she turned to him.

Every place he touched was sensitive. Every nerve in her body responded with an exquisite mounting passion, and as all sensations blurred into piercing ecstasy her last coherent thought was that, for once, Cress was going to be right.

Harlequin Plus

A WORD ABOUT THE AUTHOR

As a former journalist, Jane Donnelly reported news, interviewed celebrities and reviewed television shows. But never did she even consider fiction...until one day on a bus she overheard a girl saying to a friend, "Auntie Flo made out she didn't know he was coming, but she knew all right."

For the rest of the bus ride, Jane amused herself by imagining who "he" was and what the auntie's angle was. When she got home she wrote a little story based on the conversation and sold it. Within twelve months she was selling everything, from short thrillers to movie scripts. And then, with fifty novelettes behind her, she tried her hand at a full-length novel. The result was her first Harlequin, *A Man Apart* (Romance #1227), published in 1968.

Jane makes her home in the ancient village of Quinton, on the edge of the Cotswolds, five miles from Stratford-on-Avon—Shakespeare country! Her historic cottage was once a "witches' house," but Jane feels strongly that if any witchcraft was ever practiced there, it must have been the "white" variety—for she cannot imagine a place more filled with peace and contentment.

Enter a uniquely exciting new world with

Harlequin American Romance T.M.

Harlequin American Romances are the first romances to explore today's love relationships. These compelling novels reach into the hearts and minds of women across America... probing the most intimate moments of romance, love and desire.

You'll follow romantic heroines and irresistible men as they boldly face confusing choices. Career first, love later? Love without marriage? Long-distance relationships? All the experiences that make love real are captured in the tender, loving pages of **Harlequin American Romances.**

What makes American women so different when it comes to love? Find out with **Harlequin American Romance!**

Send for your introductory FREE book now!

Get this book FREE!

Mail to:

Harlequin Reader Service

In the U.S.
2504 West Southern Avenue
Tempe, AZ 85282

In Canada
649 Ontario Street
Stratford, Ontario N5A 6W2

YES! I want to be one of the first to discover **Harlequin American Romance.** Send me FREE and without obligation *Twice in a Lifetime.* If you do not hear from me after I have examined my FREE book, please send me the 4 new **Harlequin American Romances** each month as soon as they come off the presses. I understand that I will be billed only $2.25 for each book (total $9.00). There are no shipping or handling charges. There is no minimum number of books that I have to purchase. In fact, I may cancel this arrangement at any time. *Twice in a Lifetime* is mine to keep as a FREE gift, even if I do not buy any additional books.

Name _____ (please print)

Address _____ Apt. no. _____

City _____ State/Prov. _____ Zip/Postal Code _____

Signature (If under 18, parent or guardian must sign.)

This offer is limited to one order per household and not valid to current Harlequin American Romance subscribers. We reserve the right to exercise discretion in granting membership. If price changes are necessary, you will be notified.

Offer expires April 30, 1984   154 BPA NAC7

AR-SUB-200

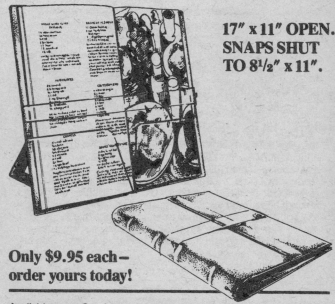